Patterns in the Sand

Tony is slowly coming to terms with the death
of his mother, but he still feels alone and very angry.
He can't understand how his dad can get his life
back together so quickly. Things with Clare aren't
what they were, and Gary and Tony are growing
apart.

There doesn't seem to be much to look forward
to – until the festival starts, and Tony meets Jodie…

Sue Mayfield lives with her family in Cheltenham
and is the author of seven books for teenagers. She
bases her stories on real-life issues and crises. When
she is not writing, she enjoys walking her dog, salsa
dancing and watching movies with her sons.

For David, Grace, Hannah,
Ned and Jono

patterns
in the
sand

Sue Mayfield

LION

A Lion Children's Book
an imprint of
Lion Hudson plc
Mayfield House, 256 Banbury Road,
Oxford OX2 7DH, England
www.lionhudson.com
ISBN 0 7459 4891 X

First published as *A Time to be Born*
by Scholastic Publications Ltd, 1995
This revised edition published by Lion Hudson, 2004
10 9 8 7 6 5 4 3 2 1 0

Acknowledgments
Scripture quotations taken from the Holy Bible, New
International Version, copyright © 1973, 1978, 1984
International Bible Society. Used by permission of Zondervan
and Hodder & Stoughton Limited. All rights reserved. The 'NIV'
and 'New International Version' trademarks are registered in
the United States Patent and Trademark Office by International
Bible Society. Use of either trademark requires the permission
of International Bible Society. UK trademark number 1448790.

A catalogue record for this book is available
from the British Library

Typeset in 11/16 Garamond ITC Lt BT
Printed and bound in Great Britain
by Cox & Wyman Ltd, Reading

There is a time for everything...
A time to be born and a time to die...
A time to weep and a time to laugh...
A time to mourn and a time to dance...
A time to scatter stones and a time to gather...

From Ecclesiastes Chapter 3

1

It's late July.

There I am, sitting on the pier, dangling my legs over the edge. I've been running and I'm panting a bit, catching my breath. My knees are pink and covered with little beads of perspiration. It's the sprinting that makes me sweat. I could go all day at a steady pace. Next year I'm going to do the Great North Run. So I've got this training circuit: along the beach the full length of the bay, up the ramp at the far end, back along the path that skirts round the clifftop, down the steps – all sixty-three of them – then a hundred-metre sprint across the hard sand. I paced it out once. It's exactly a hundred metres from the pier to the rocks that jut out in the middle of the bay, but it only works at low tide when there's a good stretch of hard sand.

My hair feels damp so I push it back off my face. It's getting really long. I'm growing it now that school's finished for the summer. They don't care how you have it in the Sixth Form and you don't have to wear uniform either. Clare keeps saying I should dye it with that henna stuff that makes it reddish. Maybe I will.

It's pretty early in the morning. The stone pier feels chilly under my bare legs. I watch the tide coming in, slopping up the beach – rearranging the sand in corrugated ridges, like ploughed earth. I like this view from the end of the pier, the way you can see the whole coastline. There are two piers – both stone – north and south of the bay. They jut out from the base of the cliffs and face each other across a stretch of open water. Beyond the south pier there are some rocks that look like long fingers of rock poking out into the sea. Then a few miles further south there's a lighthouse that crouches on a slab of rock. You can just about make out the roof of our house at the top of the cliff, tucked in beside the church steeple.

Round the edge of the bay, where the hard sand gives way to the soft whitish stuff, a man in orange overalls is gathering up Coke cans and chip wrappers, stuffing them into a black bin liner and smoothing out the sand with a rake. A cloud of gulls is circling round him, scavenging for scraps. People say they make a terrible racket but I never notice. I suppose I'm used to it – I've lived here all my life. Call me strange but I like watching the gulls. I like the patterns they make as they fly and the way their white underbellies catch the sun. They're mostly herring gulls on our beach. Last year I found a herring gull with a broken wing and looked after it until it could fly again. Whenever I watch the birds I wonder if one of them is Bono. I called him that because I like U2. Clare likes U2 as well – that was how it all started between us, back in Year 10. Before Mum died.

Wombat, my dog, is running in circles on the sand, flitting in and out of the caves, prancing from one interesting smell to another. I put two fingers between my teeth and whistle sharply. Wombat stands still and his ears – which normally flop and dangle – stand up straight like two wigwams. Then he starts running towards me, bouncing like a crazy rocking horse.

'Go, Wombat!' I shout and he splashes into the waves and wades out to where I'm sitting. He has to swim to reach the base of the steps and he gets tangled in a mass of black seaweed so that he looks as if he's been through an oil slick. Then he bounds up onto the pier and shakes himself all over me!

'Cheers, Wombat!' I say and he pokes his long wet nose into my armpit.

There's no one else on the beach – just us and the orange man, tidying up after yesterday's trippers. Soon it'll be crowded, people streaming from the car park with their cool boxes and wind breaks and body boards. I like the beach best when it's empty and quiet. But then I'm weird!

I like it in winter when it's deserted and stormy. In summer it feels different. Suddenly there's a bouncy castle along by the caves, where in winter there are only piles of driftwood and crunchy seaweed, and there's a caravan selling hot dogs and peeled shrimps in little white polystyrene cartons and a hut where you can rent orange deckchairs. And the sea is full of kids in wet suits riding on inflatable dolphins. It's a bit like an invasion – a character change. As if the beach is putting on fancy dress!

I hear the bell striking eight and picture Dad getting up and dragging on his clothes and going across to the church to unlock the huge wooden doors and say his prayers. I brush some flecks of sand off my trainers. Wombat presses his damp fur against me and wags his tail. It feels as if it's going to be a nice day. Again! It hasn't rained since my exams started. Day after day we sweated it out in the school gym, writing paper after paper. I had my last one on 17 June. Finito! No more swotting. No more GCSE coursework. Just freedom and a whole summer to myself. Not that anything exciting is likely to happen…

I'm supposed to be doing something about getting a job. Maybe today is the day to get it sorted. But I'm thinking of calling Gary to see if he fancies a bike ride. I haven't seen Gary much since we went on study leave. Come August he'll be starting his job as an apprentice plasterer. 'Life in the real world, Tones,' he says. 'Loadsa money!'

I'm staying on in the Sixth Form because I can't think

of anything else to do. I can't even decide which 'A' Levels to take. Maybe English. Maybe Geography. I'll wait and see what my results are like. I've thought about being a vet but then I'd have to do three Sciences and I totally hate Physics. Making decisions isn't my strong point.

A herring gull lands on the pier and I watch it fold its wings across its back and stand motionless, staring out across the sea, not blinking. I wonder what it's thinking about. Is it just watching for fish or does it have other thoughts? Do seagulls have to make decisions? What do you think? It's a mature bird – fully grown – two feet long with pink legs and a yellow razor bill. It isn't Bono. He has a bump on the left side of his beak and a permanently bad -tempered expression. I'd recognize him anywhere.

'If you see Bono,' I say, 'tell him Tony says Hi!' The bird flies off, plunging down into the waves. I stand up and stretch myself.

'Breakfast, Wombat,' I say and he sets off along the pier, dodging rockpools. I start jogging, jumping down onto the hard sand. I can see the crisscross tracks birds' feet have made and the trail of footprints from my earlier sprint. I sprint once more – this time across the soft sand that kills your legs – and when I reach the bottom of the cliffs I clip on Wombat's lead. He pulls like mad, straining against his collar, almost strangling himself.

'Go, Wombat!' I shout and he pulls me up the cliff path as if I were waterskiing!

2

I did go for a bike ride with Gary that day. We went along the old railway line to Prior's Dene. It turned out even hotter than I'd expected. The cinder track was baked hard and the wheels of the bikes sent clouds of black dust spraying up so that our legs were speckled with tiny smuts by the time we arrived at the river.

There's a swimming hole at Prior's Dene where the water's chest deep and dark like tea with no milk in. There's a rope swing knotted to a tree just above the deepest part of the river. Gary whipped his clothes off, swung out on the rope – Tarzan-style – and then dropped into the water in his boxer shorts. He screamed at how cold it was.

'Wimp!' I said, so he splashed me until I was as wet as he was.

We stayed by the river all afternoon – sunbathing and drinking beers and playing skimmer stones. When we got too hot, we swam – plunging into the cool brown water. Then we spread ourselves out to dry in the polleny grass. I was squinting at the sky, watching a kestrel hovering above the trees. Gary had his eyes shut and his elbows behind his head so that he looked like he had huge ears, like Yoda off Star Wars. He was prattling on about stuff – his new job, how glad he was to be finished with school, how amazing his muscles were since he'd started lifting weights at the gym, how incredibly sexy Sharon (his girlfriend) thought he was.

'Yeah sure Gary,' I said. 'You're a god! I stand in awe of you.' I didn't mean it of course. But sarcasm is wasted on Gary – he's not that subtle. He just flexed his pecs and smiled to himself. I pulled the head off some spiky grass and flicked it at his chest.

'I'm thinking of getting a tattoo,' he said. 'On my shoulder blade. A snake in the shape of S for Sharon…'

'What if she dumps you and you start going out with someone called… I don't know… Michelle?' I said.

'Why the heck would she dump me, Tony?' Gary said. I said nothing.

Gary started going out with Sharon around the same time I started seeing Clare. Except they're still together – a year later. And we're not.

We got chips on the way back and ate them sitting on a wall. Gary chucked his wrapper in someone's front garden. He's such a slob. He only did it to annoy me. As we cycled back down the coast road we passed some girls on horses and Gary started making lewd gestures and shouting obscenities at them. It was supposed to be funny but it was just embarrassing. I hate it when he does that. Treats girls as if they're stupid... and available. Assumes they all fancy him. Gary Stevens – the world's biggest babe magnet. Not!

The truth is, I don't really like Gary much these days. I guess we've drifted apart. Now we've nothing in common. Maybe we never had. We used to play football but that was about it. I only walked to school with him for five years out of habit – because he lived so close. Now it seems as though the things that made us friends are getting smaller all the time and the things that annoy me are getting bigger. Our worlds are parting. That happens as you get older. Everything changes.

3

They say that when someone dies it's the first year that is the worst – the first Christmas, the first birthday, the first anniversary of their death. When Easter came round again this year I went off for the day, by myself, on my bike. I rode for miles and when I came back I could hardly remember where I'd been. It seemed a strange coincidence that Mum died on Good Friday. I reckon she'd have liked it – dying the same day as Jesus – like being born on Christmas Day.

What I remember most from the days after she died was the silence. People don't know what to say. They avoid you because they think that any mention of what's happened might make you upset. Upset is such a stupid word – like spilling a drink – so trivial. They stay away to help you get over the shock – or so they say. It felt like we were stuck inside an envelope of silence. The house had this deathly hush – no callers, no doctors or nurses, no Betty coming in to help with Mum. It was right at the beginning of the Easter holidays. Two weeks off school and I saw almost nobody. Gary avoided me for weeks. I reckon he couldn't handle it, couldn't cope with me when I wasn't mucking about, joking around. It was as if he was scared of something. He couldn't really cope with Mum when she was alive – the wheelchair and the shaking and not being able to hear what she said clearly. Gary always seemed embarrassed by her. He never came round to my place much, we always met up at his.

So many things happened last summer. And so much changed. My leg was in plaster when Mum died. I was meant to have the plaster cast off that week anyway, but there wasn't much of it left after I'd been down on the beach and stood in the sea. It's funny stuff, plaster of Paris. It looks so hard and solid but if you get it wet it just dissolves into a mushy pulp. Not that I either noticed or cared at the time. The day Mum died was the same day that Bono was released back to the wild again. That wasn't coincidence. I think I took him down to the beach that day *because* she'd died – almost as if I needed to know he could fly. I went to the beach as soon as we got back from the hospital – it can't have been much after half past eight in the morning. She'd died at 7.50. I know that because I was watching the clock on the hospital wall. Bono was ready to fly. The vet had given his wing the all clear – it had healed really well – and he'd had a practice flight in my Geography teacher's garage the week before.

He didn't fly off immediately. The vet said he might not. He did one or two short circuits, flying a few metres across the sand, then stopping – circling, wary and unsure of himself. It was a horrible day – thick grey clouds like a blanket of doom, and no clear horizon – just black sea merging into dirty sky and rain lashing down.

When Bono finally flew out to sea I was crying so much I could hardly make him out. He lost himself quickly among other flecks of white hovering over the waves. Then I noticed Dad on the clifftop watching us. I think I waved to him and shouted something about Bono being able to fly. I can't remember it very clearly – the details are lost in a sort of fog – but I remember I was glad Dad was there – that somehow he understood, about the bird, and Mum, and me needing him to fly, to fly on wings like an eagle.

I cut what was left of the plaster off when I got home. My ankle looked really scrawny and thin and when I walked on it it felt like a stick that was about to snap. I went for lots of bike rides to build the muscles up. It felt brilliant to be able to move again. Not being able to walk properly or play football or ride my bike for over a month had almost driven me nuts.

That was when I took up running – after the plaster came off, after Mum died in the spring last year. I started going out jogging early in the morning – just short distances at first, but I found it really easy, so sometimes at weekends I'd run three or four miles – five even. Usually I went along the coast. There's a cliff path that goes about two miles and then you can cut inland and pick up a field path that runs along the edge of the golf course. I got really into it. Dad bought me a watch for my birthday that had a speedometer on it and a stopwatch. I like timing myself and working out my speed as I run. Sometimes when I run, I just blot everything out, and count strides in my head – almost like hypnotizing myself. But sometimes I find myself thinking about things – thinking about Mum, remembering her. People often say that as you die your whole life flashes in front of you. Well, it's a bit like that when someone else dies too. It's like you're watching a film of the person's life, only you watch it in bits – snatches of it here and there – and you find yourself remembering things that happened years ago – things that at the time seemed trivial and irrelevant – revisited, as if your brain was some kind of time machine.

I reckon I grew about six inches last summer. I started shaving and grew three hairs on my chest, and I won the 1500 metres at School Sports Day.

Dad and I went on holiday – just the two of us – for the first time ever. It wasn't a brilliant holiday but it was OK. In the circumstances. We were having breakfast when Dad suggested it.

'Let's go away,' he said, putting some bread in the toaster. Breakfast... that's another thing that's changed. When Mum was alive, breakfast always seemed to be a rush – Dad and I used to take turns to get Mum out of bed. We had to use an electric hoist that was fastened to the ceiling above her bed. It lifted her up and swung her – feet dangling – across the gap between her bed and the wheelchair. She couldn't really use her limbs at all towards the end. We had to wash her, and take her to the toilet, and feed her and everything. I suppose it's kind of strange to do those sorts of things for your mum. They're the things she does for you when you're a baby only you don't remember when you're big. I was so used to it though. I did it all without thinking.

After she died and we didn't have all that to do: breakfast time always seemed quite leisurely. Dad would read the paper and sometimes I left it till the morning to finish homework. We used to have the radio on to fill the silence. Dad likes Radio 4 so we took turns – one day his choice, the next day Virgin FM. We've got quite good at sorting out things like that. In fact we get on better generally than I ever would have thought.

I poured myself a second bowl of Shreddies.

'Where to?' I said. We'd never had a proper holiday as long as I could remember. Sometimes we'd go to stay with friends, or we'd go to special hotels that catered for disabled people, but they weren't usually in very exciting places. Anyway, the effort of taking all Mum's clobber meant it never seemed like a holiday. Mum didn't cope very well with changes to her routine. She'd cry a lot and Dad would come back looking exhausted and grey.

'Where do you fancy?' Dad said.

I thought for a moment. Clare had gone to France with her Mum and her older sister. They'd gone for four weeks to stay in a gite. I was missing her like mad. They'd actually invited me to go too but I felt as if I couldn't leave Dad. Not for a whole month. Not yet. Some days, back then – last summer – he went about as if he was in a trance or stoned or something. And he'd forget things…

We decided on Scotland – or rather, an island off the coast of Scotland called Arran. I'd have liked to go somewhere hotter – Corfu maybe, or Majorca (Gary's family always go there) but Dad hates flying and I hate crowded beaches, so we settled for wilderness.

'Let's camp,' Dad said. 'Get back to basics. Rough it a bit.' So we bought some gear. We bought a tent… and a stove… and a gas lantern… and two new cocoon-style sleeping bags… and a water carrier… and plastic bowls… spoons… knives… and (best of all) a Swiss Army knife.

'And fly repellent!' Dad said suddenly as we stood by the cash desk. 'To keep the midges away!' He was busy writing a cheque. I found two cans of mosquito spray and added them to the ever growing pile beside the till. I couldn't believe the amount of stuff he was buying! Dad always used to be a bit stingy. Then, after Mum died, he started spending money as if it was going out of fashion, always buying things – for the house, for me. One day I came home from school and he'd bought me the new U2 album. Just bought it and put it on my bed. Like it was my birthday or something.

We had to go on a ferry to get to Arran. The sea was choppy and I was seasick. I threw up over the side with two girls watching me and giggling. One of the girls looked like Gary's girlfriend Sharon. She had the same frothy hair, the same skin-tight clothes, the same trying-too-hard-to-be-sexy look which Gary seems to go for. Gary reckoned he and Sharon were sleeping together all through Year Eleven. He could have been lying. Gary makes things up when he wants to impress people. But then, he and Sharon were always disappearing from school at lunchtime and coming back with love bites all over their necks… so they must have been doing something!

I was glad – after my bout of nausea – when we drove the car off the ferry onto solid ground again. We headed south to a spot called Kildonan where there was a pub, three holiday cottages and a tiny campsite, just spitting distance from the beach. It was raining slightly when we arrived and it didn't look too promising. But Dad was undaunted.

'The rain won't last long,' he said cheerfully. 'We'll wait for it to stop and pitch in the dry.' So we went into the pub and Dad bought two pints of lager and a bag of crisps. We played pool – very badly. Dad kept getting the angles wrong and bouncing the balls off the cushions and I wasn't much better. Two surly-looking locals sat at the bar tapping coins on the woodwork as a hint that they were waiting for us to finish our game.

Later on it stopped raining – briefly – and we managed to put up the tent. Inside, it was cosy enough but I didn't sleep much the first night. The ground felt hard and lumpy and every noise seemed amplified ten times over. When it began to rain again it sounded like bullets on a tin roof. Beside me – *right* beside me, too close for comfort – Dad was snoring and muttering to himself. I lay in my cocoon, feeling cold. To warm myself up I thought about Clare – thought about her soft dark hair, falling messily about her shoulders, her freckly nose, the smell of her skin. 'I'll send you a postcard from Scotland,' I'd said, the day she went to France. 'Only *one?*' she'd said with a flash of a smile. Then she'd kissed me.

The morning after the first night, I was glad to get out of the tent and stretch myself. The sky had cleared and there was a pale watery sun which was still low enough to catch on the sea and flash like ice. I went for a walk on the beach. It was much stonier than at home with just a tiny crescent of white sand. There were no cliffs, just grey rocks which straggled out into the water in untidy piles. I walked to a high, jutting rock and sat throwing stones out of a rockpool into the sea. There was a fresh, salty smell that was familiar and yet somehow different – cleaner than at home, and wilder.

Just offshore there was a line of low black rocks, like threaded beads. I watched them for ages, absent-mindedly, thinking about something else. As I looked, one of them seemed to move, to change shape. Its roundness became more pointed, then it disappeared altogether, sliding into the water. I stared hard. Another moved, wobbled a bit, grew taller, then settled back, blob-like again. The more I looked, the more it seemed as if all the stones were moving. I jumped up and ran back to the tent. Dad was just emerging through the flap, rubbing sleep from his eyes.

'Dad!' I shouted. 'Get the binoculars! There's something moving on the rocks!' It was seals, dozens of them. Through the powerful lenses of Dad's binoculars I could make out their faces – moist-eyed and dog-like, with enormous whiskers and sleepy smiles. I wrote a postcard to Clare later that day.

Dear Clare,
Hi! Threw up on the boat and hardly slept last night –
ground a bit hard!!! But saw real live seals on the

beach this morning. WOW'!!!
Missing you heaps and stacks!
Love and kisses (lots of them!!!)
T xxxxxxxxxxx

We moved, halfway through the week, up to the north of the island. It was more mountainous there, and wilder. Inland, there were tiny lochs with deep blue water and hazy purple heather and dragonflies everywhere, buzzing at shoulder height.

We did a lot of walking – up hills, and around the rocks of the coast, and through thick forests to waterfalls – zig-zagging about the island. Dad cooked porridge and fried eggs and corned beef hash on the stove and, one night, I cooked some fish on a wood fire.

We didn't say very much to each other. Dad's not that easy to talk to. Several times I wanted to talk about Mum. There were things I wanted to ask him, things I'd never understood. Sometimes I just wanted to mention her so that it felt like she was there too. There was a gap, a hole. I kept wanting to put her into it. But I didn't say anything, and neither did Dad. Maybe he needed space in his head. Maybe we both did.

One day a whole herd of red deer ran across the hillside where we were walking. We stood still and watched them go past. I don't know if they saw us. I spent a lot of time watching birds through the binoculars, and

Dad read a lot of books. I even tried drawing, but I wasn't much good at it – not without a picture to copy.

At one campsite a boy of about twelve tried to teach me to juggle with three tennis balls. His name was Richard and he had a black dog called Bouncer. I sat in the sandy grass at the mouth of his tent, passing the balls from hand to hand until my head was spinning – but I still couldn't do it.

It was on the last day that we saw the eagle. At first I thought it was just another buzzard. We were high up – over a thousand metres above sea level. It was a clear day and from where we were you could see the whole island. The bird was hovering above a peak of rock at the summit – just hanging there, wings outstretched. The only eagle I'd ever seen was a stuffed one in a museum we went to on a school trip. I'd seen them on TV as well, but that gives you no idea of the size. I watched it carefully. It was huge – dark brown, with wing tips spread like fingers. Too big to be a buzzard. And not the right shape. I reached for Dad's binoculars and just as I focussed the lenses on it, it turned sideways, so that I could see its head and beak in profile. It was a Golden Eagle. I watched it for ages, training the glasses on it – following the circles of its flight, watching it swoop and glide – so effortless, so powerful.

When it had moved out of sight I looked at Dad and there were tears streaming down his face. I went off by myself and sat on a rock looking at the island. I didn't feel especially sad. All I felt was a terrible emptiness.

That night I wrote another postcard.

Dear Clare,
Today I saw a golden eagle – soaring!! Wow!
Wish you'd been here too.
Love, Tony x

4

I knew Clare would understand about the eagle. She's the only person that knows, apart from Dad. I've had this thing about eagles for a while, because of Mum really. She had this favourite bit in the Bible about soaring like an eagle. I can remember it by heart – 'Those who hope in the Lord will renew their strength... they will rise up on wings like eagles...' Mum used to say that dying would be like that – like being picked up on the back of a huge bird and flying everywhere, looking down at things, and being able to go wherever you pleased. She hated not being able to move and having to depend on people to get anywhere. I did a picture for her the Christmas before she died. It wasn't that good. I copied it from an encyclopedia at the library. It was a golden eagle flying over a lake. I got the markings on the feathers quite well – all the shades of brown. At the bottom I wrote the Bible reference – Isaiah 40 verse 31. I had it framed for her and she kept it beside her bed because she said it made her feel hopeful.

Clare knows lots of things about me. We're pretty close. She was my first proper girlfriend, the first girl I kissed. Clare's not like other girls at school. She's really thoughtful, she understands things. She's nice-looking too – in an unconventional sort of way. I wasn't sure if she fancied me at first. I thought maybe she was just being friendly, just feeling sorry for me. Poor Tony Sharp, the vicar's kid with a sick mother. Gary said it was obvious she liked me – that he could tell from the look on her face. But since when has Gary ever been right about anything?

After Mum died, Clare was about the only person I wanted to see. I phoned her as soon as I got back from the beach and she came straight round and stayed all day. We lay on my bed, just holding each other, me crying till my face was raw. I kept kissing her over and over, feeling as if I wanted to lose myself in her. I needed her so much it hurt.

I don't remember much about the first few weeks. People say that after someone dies you go numb for a while. Clare would come and we'd go for long walks along the clifftops after school, wrapped around each other. And then we'd go back to her house. I started doing my homework at Clare's, sitting curled up in her bean bag or lying on her bedroom floor, stretched out with my books – and always music on in the background. I remember listening to a lot of music. Clare is the only person I know who likes U2 as much as I do. But she likes other stuff as well. Reggae and jazz and offbeat African stuff – the sort of music her mum's into. I like her mum. She used to cook us things like spaghetti with lots of wine in the sauce and vegetarian beany stuff that gave you wind. 'Arty farty food' Gary would have called it. Gary never liked Clare much. She's way too sophisticated for him. Gary likes his women tarty and stupid with big boobs. When I was going out with Clare he'd say things like 'She's a bit flat-chested, Tones – not much to get hold of there!' and 'Have you two done it yet, Tones, or doesn't she let you?'

I never answered him. I never really told Gary anything about me and Clare. He wouldn't have understood.

I thought I was in love with Clare. In fact I felt like I'd never love anyone else in quite the same way. It sounds really cheesy but Clare made me feel happy at a time when I felt as if I'd never be happy again. Looking back, it was all a bit unreal. The happiness was artificial – like the high you get if you drink too much to forget about something.

Sex sort of crept up on us – on me anyway. Maybe I'm dead naive but I hadn't wanted things to go any further. I fancied Clare all right, and I liked touching her when we kissed – exploring the shape of her inside her clothes. Once we were lying on her bed, supposed to be doing our

Maths homework, and I slipped my hand inside her school blouse and felt her breasts. She didn't try to stop me. If anything she kissed me harder. That felt pretty good. She'd touched me too, through the outside of my jeans. That made me really want her.

But it was mostly just snogging. I hate that word – it sounds so unromantic. It's a Gary sort of word – but I can't think of a better one. It was more than just kissing – more total, more intense. But not *much* more. Not then. Not before the holidays. Not until *this* happened...

It's August, last year.

We meet in the park beside our favourite bench – the one overlooking the boating lake, next to the bush with red flowers. It's evening but still quite hot. Clare is sitting with her legs stretched out across the path and her ankles crossed. She's wearing baggy shorts and sandals and her legs look brown and longer than ever. I'm fresh back from Scotland, clutching a teddy with a tartan bow. Clare is just back from France, sporting a new hair cut – shorter than before and cut straight, level with her chin.

'Very French,' I say. 'Very chic.'

She does a twirl. 'Ooh la la!' she says in a silly French accent. Clare's good at French. I bet she gets an A*.

She looks different – older somehow – and totally gorgeous. I sit down beside her and she kisses me – first soft and then harder. 'Thanks for the postcards,' she says and I smile.

'How was France?' I ask. I put my arm around her bare shoulder. It feels warm and smooth.

'Very French, very chic!' she says and we laugh. She runs her hand across my arm and says, 'You're surprisingly brown. Was it hot in Scotland?'

'No, it's wind burn,' I say. 'It was freezing!'

'And did you use your Swiss Army knife?' she says.

'I certainly did! I gutted fish with it!' I say and I laugh like an extra in a horror film.

'Yuck,' says Clare and she pushes my hand off her shoulder.

'Not only did I gut the fish but I cooked them on a wood fire that I'd built myself. Be impressed!' I say.

'I suppose you made the flames by rubbing two sticks together, too,' she says and she starts tickling me. I tickle her back and she thrashes her legs and squeals. Then I kiss her again, long and slow, with my eyes shut. When I open my eyes she's looking at me with a deep gaze, as if she can see inside me.

'I love you,' she whispers. It's the first time she's said it and it makes me want to cry. I wish I could say it back – I think it – but the words stick in my throat. I've only said these words once before – ever. That was to Mum, just before she died, sitting in the hospital room, surrounded by curtains with tulips on them. She gave me the drawing of the eagle – the one I did for her – and said she wanted me to have it. I buried my face in the white sheet so she wouldn't see me crying.

How can I love Clare as much that, I think? How can I love her more? Using the same words doesn't seem right. There should be some different words. Different words for different kinds of love.

Clare looks disappointed that I haven't said *anything* so I stroke the back of her neck with my fingers. Then we walk. We walk a long way – first along the sand, then along the cliff path, which is dry and dusty from the hot weather. The ground has cracked like old china and where there is normally mud, there are hard peaks of trodden earth, like moon rock. Round the headland, where the lighthouse juts out into the sea, there are some sand dunes that run along the top of the next beach. Steep banks of sand dip down into a honeycomb of hollows and there's lots of that sharp grass, the stuff that cuts your legs. By the time we reach the dunes the light is beginning to fade and the whole place seems deserted and secret.

We stand silently, hand in hand on the cliff top, staring at the sea. I can hear the soft lapping sound of the waves, and a gull crying.

Suddenly, breaking the stillness, I shout 'Go!' and I run, skidding and slithering down the sandy ski slope, dragging Clare after me. It's pretty steep down there. We build up speed and pitch forward, floundering in the soft, deep sand at the bottom. Clare is squealing with laughter. I fall on my side and roll the last bit like a rolypoly – like I did when I was a kid. Clare throws herself on top of me, roaring like a tiger. I growl back and bare my teeth and we roll and tickle each other like cubs or something.

Then suddenly we're lying very still, Clare on top of me, propped on her arms with her legs either side of my waist. She's staring down at me, smiling, and the tips of her hair are brushing my face. We're at the bottom of a dip, inches deep in yellow sand. I pull her face towards me and kiss her hungrily. A month apart from her has made her lips taste like food to a starving man. She is running her lips across my face and neck and pressing all of herself against me. We roll over in the sand, touching and clasping each other deliciously until Clare pulls me onto her and says, 'Tony, I want you. I want you so much. Let's make love...'

Then I stop kissing her and freeze. She misreads the look on my face and says, 'It's OK... I've got some condoms...'

That's so Clare. Little Miss Practical.

But it's not that. I don't know why, but suddenly I'm not turned on any more. In fact, I feel terrified – paralysed almost. I roll off her, more abruptly than I mean to, and slump down into the sand beside her. Clare looks confused. I don't blame her. I try to speak...

'Clare... I... we...' I'm struggling for words. I don't even know what I want to say.

'We can't... I can't...' I say feebly. Call me stupid but

I never expected things to move this fast. I don't want things to change.

'There's no one here to see us,' Clare says. She takes hold of my hand, hesitantly, as though she's no longer sure of the ground she's on. As though the sand is shifting.

'It's not that,' I say. 'It's just... I don't want to... well, not yet... anyway, not here... it just seems...' I look at Clare but she isn't getting me.

'Seems what?' she says accusingly. Her eyes look angry. Like I've really hurt her.

'Oh God, I don't know!' I say. Nothing I say is going to make this better. She wanted to. I didn't. It's not really the sort of thing you can compromise over. It's mutual consent or nothing, isn't it? I put my head in my hands and run my fingers through my hair. Suddenly the sand feels cold and damp through my clothes.

'I'm just surprised... sort of caught unawares...' I say dumbly. Clare looks disbelieving.

'Surprised?' she says. 'Are you serious? I really love you Tony. I thought I'd made that pretty obvious!'

I can see she's crying. Clare hardly ever cries. It's usually me. She draws her knees up close to her chin and hugs them tightly, like a child.

'I thought you loved me too,' she says, sniffing.

I don't say anything. I do love her... but sex just seems so total, so, well, final... and so adult! I think of Gary and imagine his mocking laugh, taking the mick out of me.

'Wazzup Tones? Aren't you up to it? Go on, give her one! She's asking for it!'

Gary talks about sex as if it's no big deal. It's just something you do. Like going for a curry!

I start thinking about Mum and that makes it worse. Why do all my thoughts go back to her? I wish I could talk to her – ask her advice. Mum really liked Clare. And she was like her in a lot of ways. Maybe *that's* the problem. Maybe Clare is too similar to my mum. That's weird!

I put my hand out to touch Clare's arm but she flinches like a wounded animal.

'If you didn't want to do it you had a pretty funny way of showing it!' she says. Now she's really crying.

'Clare,' I say, pleading with her. I want everything to be like it was before – uncomplicated.

'I... it's not... look of *course* I wanted to... but it's just... we're so *young*... Clare, we're only fifteen!'

Clare stands up and starts to scramble back up the dunes towards the road. As she walks, soft sand avalanches downwards from each footprint. She shouts back at me, 'Well, sorr-ee! I didn't realize I was going out with someone so *immature*!'

I'm about to answer when she adds,

'Don't bother to catch me up – I'll get a bus home!'

When I get to the top of the cliffs she's gone. I pick up a stone and hurl it back down the slope. It bounces a few times and then lodges itself in the sand.

'Shit!' I say loudly. You know, when I was ten a woman from church went to see my dad to complain that she'd heard me say 'Shit' in the street. Like she thought he'd care! How petty is that? So is *that* my problem – being a vicar's kid. Is that why I can't handle the idea of sex? Am I a freak or something? Too many hang-ups? Perhaps Clare's right. Perhaps I'm just dead immature.

It's getting pretty dark by now and I'm worrying about Clare walking home by herself. I'm also worrying that I've blown it permanently. Is this it? The end of a beautiful relationship? For a moment, as I walk quickly along the dark promenade, it seems as if nothing is real – as if the last few months have been some kind of strange dream. What if none of it really happened? What if I'm actually a little kid again and Mum hasn't died? Then I remember Good Friday and the wailing ache inside me and Clare not minding that I soaked her clothes with crying. Maybe I've just needed her too much. Maybe I don't love her at all. Maybe things only happened because Clare was there and she took the pain away. Maybe… maybe…

I'm confused, that's for sure. But I'm certain about one thing. I don't feel ready to have sex with Clare. Not yet. And not on a beach, carried away in the heat of the moment. I want it to be right. The right time. Gary's wrong. Sex is a big deal – it's like you're giving yourself away, like it will change you, change everything, like you'll be a different person afterwards. 'And the two shall become one flesh...' Those words come into my head. I must have heard them in church. They must be from the Bible. Two bodies, one unit – like fusing something together, sealing it.

When I get home Dad is sitting at the kitchen table eating a bowl of cornflakes and reading the sport pages of the paper.

'You're early,' he says.

'Clare had to be home by ten,' I lie.

'Are you OK?' He looks at me over his newspaper and I reckon he guesses I'm not. I flirt with telling him what's happened. I wonder how he'll react if I ask his advice? What if I ask him whether he had sex with other women than Mum? What would he say? Just the thought of Dad having sex at all is excruciatingly embarrassing. So I look away and open the biscuit tin.

'I'm fine,' I say. That's what I used to say when people asked how Mum was all the time. Fine's a useful word. It gets people off our case. I stuff a custard cream in my mouth and say 'Is there anything on telly?'

5

There was a letter on the doorstep the day after that – green envelope, Clare's handwriting. I felt a bit sick when I saw it – the way you feel when you've broken something and you don't want to own up. I took the envelope back to bed and read it in secret. It was quite short.

Dear Tony,
You must think I'm a real cow. I made a fool of myself
last night, didn't I? I'm really sorry. I thought it was
what you wanted – what boys wanted, anyway. And
I thought a lot about it – about you – in France. I
thought it was what I wanted, too – but now I'm not
so sure.
*   I'm sorry I ran off but I couldn't handle it. You*
looked really angry. Will you still be my friend??
I suppose things have got a bit intense too fast. I've been

thinking, maybe we should see less of each other for a while – just be friends??

If you're still speaking to me will you ring me this afternoon?

I really care about you, Tony. You're very special. Yours, with lots of love, Clare xxxx

It was a relief to know she didn't hate me. I did ring her and we went for a walk – up by the golf course – with Clare's dog. Clare cried a bit and I talked about Mum and tried to explain how I felt. She's a good mate. I reckon she understands me better than anyone. But things did change after that. They cooled off. We were less involved, less wrapped up in each other. And we cut out the snogging. Now – a year later – we're just friends. Maybe closer than friends – maybe more like brother and sister.

I found Clare's letter just the other day when I was looking for my Swiss Army knife. It was in the drawer beside my bed – all crumpled up and coffee stained. Reading it again made all that stuff in the dunes seems a long time ago. It's weird how time has a way of making things that were a big deal when they happened seem a bit ridiculous afterwards. Is that what people mean when they say Time is a healer?

I needed the knife to cut some rope to tie a plank to

the bottom of the garden gate! Sounds weird, huh? The thing is... we've been having trouble with Wombat. He keeps escaping from the garden and the other day a woman brought him back from the golf course. One of these days he'll go under a bus. Dad was shouting up the stairs at me.

'Can't you do something about him, Tony? He's going to kill himself on that road...' Dad was at the bottom of the stairs, a mug of coffee in his hands. Wombat was skulking in the hallway looking ashamed of himself.

I yelled back, 'I know! It's because he can get under the gate. There's a plank in the garage and some rope – I'm going to tie it across the bottom – like a barrier... I'm just looking for my knife... Can you make sure he stays in the kitchen till I've finished?'

I was rummaging in the drawer beside my bed. I found a huge pile of tatty football cards – the sort you stick in a book and swap at school. There were three David Beckhams from his girlie hair phase. One of them had a moustache and glasses drawn on with black biro. Then I found Clare's letter and got distracted reading it.

I found the knife eventually, under a jumble of magazines. I opened the blades one by one and wiped them on my sleeve. Some of them were stiff and wouldn't budge. I tugged at them, but I haven't got any fingernails because I bite them so I couldn't get hold of the metal properly. I could hear Dad in the kitchen shouting at

Wombat. I think Dad's had second thoughts about getting a dog. Wombat was supposed to be company for us – to make the house seem less empty after Mum died. In fact he's just a pest.

Getting a dog was Cath's idea. I've never known anyone have so much influence over Dad. I wish I could persuade him to do things as easily as Cath can.

I first met Cath last October, during half term, two months after we went to Arran. Dad wanted to go on a conference in London with a load of other vicars.

'Why don't you come with me?' he said. 'Not to the conference, obviously... but to London. It would be a nice break for you. You could do some sight-seeing...'

I'd never been to London before. Dad and Mum were at college there – that's where they met – so it was familiar ground for them – hallowed ground almost.

'That's where I used to write my essays,' Dad said, pointing to a big white building with loads of windows.

'And just along there, there was a nice café... goodness, what was it called? Rosie's! That was it... I once took Alison – your mum – there... She wasn't interested in me at the time. She was going out with some music student... part German, he was...'

Dad's voice trickled away and got drowned out by the traffic. He had this far away look, as though he was lost in all the memories – like the past was more real than now.

We were walking down a wide street with lots of big

bookshops on it. Taxis went by – loads of them – like fat, black beetles. I tried to picture Mum and Dad having tea in a café. What did they look like? How old would they be? Eighteen, nineteen – not much older than I am now. I've got a photo of Mum at that age – leaning on a fence in a big sun hat. She's got long dark hair, and freckles, and a really likeable grin. I can't remember her looking anything like that – all the pictures in my head are of her ill, and pale, and dead…

We stayed in some university halls of residence, south of the river. It was pretty sleazy – lots of traffic noise and grimy buildings and litter. From what I saw I couldn't decide if I liked London or not.

I liked the Underground – especially the maps, like multi-coloured spaghetti, and all the escalators, and tunnels like rabbit burrows. I liked the big adverts in all the stations and the sudden hissing draught when a train came.

Dad gave me a map and he put yellow marker pen dots on things like Buckingham Palace, and the Houses of Parliament, and the Tower of London – and circled the Tube stations I'd need to use to get to them. I hardly saw Dad in the three days we were there – just at breakfast times and then again in the evenings. He seemed to be having a good time – he said he'd met up with some old friends who were on the conference too.

On the Thursday it was raining. I wanted to go to

Madame Tussaud's so I took the tube to Baker Street, Northern Line to Charing Cross, and then the brown one – Bakerloo – to Baker Street. At Baker Street station there were tiles with Sherlock Holmes on them as you came up the escalator.

There was a queue to get into Madame Tussaud's. I bought some popcorn and waited in the foyer. There was a photobooth where you could have your picture taken with Muhammad Ali or Kylie or Elton John. The photos looked quite realistic. I wondered if there was a waxwork of Bono. Maybe I'd have my picture taken next to *him*. Then I saw how much it cost and changed my mind. Money goes nowhere in London. Dad had given me forty quid but it was disappearing fast. Food seemed to cost a fortune and I kept paying too much on the Underground because I couldn't work out the fare system.

Eventually I paid and went through a heavy door into a corridor carpeted with expensive blue plush. Behind the door a doorman in a braided uniform was holding out his hand for my ticket. I fumbled in my pockets for a moment before I realized he was wax! Feeling stupid – and hoping no one had seen me – I followed the crowd into the Hall of Fame. There was Tom Cruise and Julia Roberts and Graham Norton and Posh and Becks. At first the models were convincing, but the more you stared, the more phoney they looked. Some of them weren't quite right – the face was too narrow, or the eyes were wrong, or the lips – but all of them just looked… well, like wax – not alive.

I remembered a conversation I'd had with Clare before Mum died. Clare had seen her grandma after she was dead, laid out in her coffin – all rouged up and in a frilly blouse. She said her gran had looked like a waxwork. I thought of Mum and shuddered. These waxworks didn't really look like she had. They were too shiny, too glossy, too artificial.

After the Hall of Fame there was the Palace – all red carpets and gold trim. The royal family were standing posed in front of a curtain with a coat of arms on it. The queen didn't look much like the real thing, but Charles was good – especially the nose – and the corgis were pretty lifelike. I kept going and passed Britney, who looked as if she was winking at me (I wish!). Then I was in a dark corridor and I could hear spooky music. A sign to 'The Chamber of Horrors' pointed to a dark doorway. I didn't fancy it much but I was being jostled by the crowd. Trying to stop was like trying to stand still in a fast-flowing river. Suddenly I was looking at severed heads and guillotine blades encrusted with blood and matted chunks of hair. There was the 'Brides in the Bath' killer, standing over the tin bath where he'd drowned his wife, and a woman in a long black dress dangling from a hangman's noose. A serial killer sat slumped in an electric chair under fierce white lights and someone else was facing a firing squad. Every couple of minutes there was a loud crack of gunfire and the model jerked sideways in the chair. Then the head was yanked upright again – you could see the strings – and his lifeless eyes were staring – staring at crowds of Japanese tourists. I felt sick.

I overtook the crowds and walked quickly along a corridor past Ant and Dec and the Incredible Hulk and burst through the revolving doors. It felt good to be out in the rain again.

St Paul's Cathedral wasn't much better. I got the tube to a station called Bank and arrived as the clock was striking two. There were twenty-four slate steps up to a huge doorway with tall pillars either side. Then there was a flash-looking revolving door made of grey smoked glass. That surprised me. It looked more like a department store than a church. Beyond the door a woman was sitting at a cash register and a sign said *Admission £7.00*. I thought about my dwindling cash. £7.00 seemed a bit steep just to see an old church – but I wanted to go in. Then I remembered how once at York Minster Dad got in free by saying he was going to pray. It was worth a try. I cleared my throat and said in my poshest voice, 'I only want to come in and pray for a few minutes.'

The woman smiled warmly at me as though she was impressed.

'If you go round to the side door, love, and explain, they'll let you in there,' she said. I glanced back and saw that she was still smiling at me. I reckon I made her day.

At the side entrance there was another revolving door and a man in a long black cape who looked like he was standing guard. He was talking to a group of tourists so I sneaked past him and entered the spinning smoked glass, but as I did so the cloaked figure caught me by the arm and said accusingly, 'Are you going to pray?'

I said I was, and wondered if God would strike me dead for lying. Just inside the door there was one of those ropes they use in museums for keeping you out of the interesting bits. A notice pointed left into a little side room. *Reserved for Private Prayer* it said. I ignored it and walked past into the main part of the cathedral.

It was massive. It felt even bigger on the inside than it had seemed from the street. The floor was like a giant chess board and the ceiling – like the roof of a huge high tunnel – was painted with gold angels. There seemed to be tombs everywhere – enormous things with the sleek carved figures of dead people laid on top. I touched one of them. It was hard and cold.

Walking nearer to the altar, which was ablaze with candles, I looked up at the inside of the dome. It seemed to stretch for miles. Far away on the roof I could just make out shadowy pictures of horses and trees and fat women half-undressed and strange creatures with wings. They looked like faded black-and-white photographs. And there was Jesus, with gold hair and a crown – holding up hands with the marks of nails in them. He seemed to be staring down at me – staring, but not smiling.

I shuddered again, as I had in Madame Tussaud's. Everywhere I could hear the strange muffled sound of footsteps and hushed voices lost in a vacuum of space and silence. Everywhere there seemed to be Death.

I slipped out of the door I'd come in and caught a bus that was going to Oxford Circus. The bus was crowded and a Cockney conductor was cracking jokes in a loud voice. I stared out of the windows, recognizing places from the TV and from playing Monopoly... Fleet Street... Pall Mall... Regent Street... Picadilly Circus.

Once, the traffic stopped at some lights and a police van screamed past with its siren wailing and the blue light flashing. Leaning in the doorway at the back of the bus the conductor said, 'That's the geyser stuck his wife in the acid bath. He's being tried at the Old Bailey this week. That's them taking 'im back to Brixton. They aren't taking no chances.'

He pronounced 'chances' as though it had an 'r' in it. I thought of the Chamber of Horrors.

After waxworks and marble tomb figures Cath seemed incredibly alive – almost disgustingly alive – like turning the light on too bright when you've been used to the gloom. She was small, with short greying hair and big earrings and she talked quickly, waving her hands about a lot as she spoke. We were sitting in a crowded Italian restaurant she'd taken us to, near Oxford Circus. I felt a bit spaced-out after the day I'd had. I don't think I said much. The spaghetti was hard to eat without slurping and I kept splattering drops of tomato sauce down the front of my shirt. I noticed that Dad was smiling a lot and cracking jokes. Dad, apparently, had known Cath years ago – they'd been friends at college. I wondered why I'd never heard of her before. Maybe Mum didn't like her.

Cath lived in North London in a place that sounded, from hearing her talk, as if everyone there had either been raped, mugged, or in prison! She was a vicar too, but the sort of things she seemed to spend her time doing didn't sound much like Dad's job. She was talking about counselling and therapy and victim-support groups, whereas Dad spends most of his life visiting old ladies with cats and nice china.

I wasn't sure I liked Cath at first. Something about her made me a bit suspicious. Maybe it was Dad – the way he sucked up to her all the time, all soppy and giggly. He was never like that with Mum. Sometimes I used to think he didn't love Mum at all – that he was just going through the motions, doing what he knew he had to do. Cath asked me lots of questions about school and football and running and what I thought of London. I said I thought it was filthy. Dad drank a lot of wine and we all ate big ice creams. And then Cath had to go. She squeezed my hand as she picked up her briefcase. It was a conspiratorial sort of squeeze, as if we had a secret. Dad kissed her on the cheek and I heard him say, 'I'll be in touch'.

6

'Being in touch' is putting it mildly. The week after we came back from London, Dad never seemed to be off the phone. He was kind of on a high – all talkative and jolly and crashing around the house like a deranged elephant. He's big, my Dad – six foot three with size eleven feet and when he runs downstairs you certainly hear him coming. When Mum was alive we had to creep round a lot because she slept in the afternoons, so we got into the habit of being quiet. I'm a total expert at going upstairs without making a sound. You have to avoid the stair third from the bottom and the one second from the top because they squeak and there's a loose floor board on the landing outside Mum and Dad's room that makes a noise like a frog croaking if you stand on it!

Like I said, it was Cath's idea that we got Wombat. She suggested it during one of their cosy late night chats, Dad crouching in the hall with his back to the radiator and a mug of cocoa in his hand.

He was full of it next morning.

'I've been thinking,' he said, 'maybe we should get a dog.'

He told me what Cath had said about the need for new interests and 'bonding' after bereavement – the necessity of refocussing the household when someone, whose illness has been long term, isn't there any more. Cath, so it seemed, was something of an expert in bereavement and death. She ran courses on it.

I was a bit annoyed at Dad for letting himself be talked into it so easily. Whenever I've mentioned getting a pet before, he's refused point blank. But I was pleased about the dog because I'd always wanted a dog.

We went to the RSPCA shelter. Dad said we might as well adopt a stray as buy some expensive pedigree thing. A dog was a dog after all – it ate and yapped and went to the toilet a lot! The shelter made me feel sick. There were so many dogs. I wanted to bring home half a dozen.

'It's twice as bad after Christmas,' the bloke said. He was showing us round. There were rows of dogs, in pens, behind a wire barrier. They were looking out with terrible sad eyes. We passed a miserable-looking Alsatian, standing with its back to us, quivering at the sound of our feet and voices, and not daring to look round.

'He's been beaten, that one 'as,' the man said. 'His hind

quarters were all striped when he came in. Bit neurotic he is too – not surprisingly…'

There was a funny-looking Dalmatian that was all white apart from a few black splodges on its face.

'He looks as if he's lost his spots in the wash,' Dad said. I liked the thought of a dog that was a bit unusual.

When we reached Wombat's pen he was sitting right beside the fence and when he saw us coming he bounced up and down and grinned a doggy grin. He looked a bit loopy but the way he threw himself at us, it would have been impossible not to choose him.

That was last November. He was ridiculously friendly from the word go. I cradled him in the back seat of the car and he squirmed and wriggled, trying to turn round and lick my face. He was small enough to carry and was covered in soft woolly fur that dropped out all over the carpet in the first week we had him. We got him a bed and put it in the utility room, where Bono's chicken wire run had been. I put newspaper all over the floor to soak up his wee, but he just chewed it up and trod pellets of shredded newsprint all over the house.

Right from the start Wombat was a nuisance. He likes to jump over things and to dig holes and just lately he's become obsessed with escaping from the garden. I can't bring myself to tie him up, as if he was a vicious Rottweiler or something – like the one I used to call 'The Beast' at a house I used to go to on my paper round. (I would stay outside the gate until it had seen me, just in case it wasn't fastened up. When it heard the gate it would go crazy, rushing at me and barking till the chain was stretched to its fullest extent and it was almost throttling itself. Then I'd rush in, praying that the chain wouldn't snap!)

I can't imagine Wombat going for anyone – he's too much of a nice guy! – but his Houdini routines are getting tedious. Tying a plank across the bottom of the gate looked as if it would help a bit but there was still a hole in the hedge that he could squeeze through. I was wondering how I could block the gap when I had an idea.

'Chicken wire,' I said, out loud. This was last Thursday. We were in the kitchen.

'What about it?' said Dad. He was rummaging in the cupboard under the sink, pulling out metal baking tins and those wire racks you put cakes on when they come out of the oven.

'There's that roll we had for Bono's pen – in the garage,' I said. 'If I pegged it across the front of the hedge it would block the hole, wouldn't it? Have we got any wire cutters?' My mind was running ahead, planning how I'd do it.

'Chicken wire!' said Dad standing up. He said it as if chicken wire had just been invented, and then he said, 'Is it strong enough to stand fifty sausages on?'

I looked at him in amazement. His hair was all over the place. Sometimes he looks completely shot away.

'What?' I said.

'Or would it buckle with the heat?' Dad said.

He looked miles away. I could tell he hadn't been listening to me. He was thinking about something else.

'What are you talking about, Dad?' I asked.

'The barbecue,' he said, 'in the garden. If we build towers of bricks, we can spread chicken wire across the top and put the charcoal underneath. That'll work, won't it?'

I was really confused now.

'What barbecue, Dad?'

Dad was washing his hands in the sink and rubbing them briskly on a blue towel.

'For the Beach Festival Team – the welcome party – when they all get here…' he said.

When he said Beach Festival I remembered very vaguely that Dad had said something about a bunch of teenagers from somewhere else coming to do some special events on the beach in the summer – something to do with church. It was ages since he'd mentioned it and I hadn't really been listening at the time. I tend to blank out stuff about church, like it's nothing to do with me. Because it isn't – not any more.

'When are they coming?' I asked. I was stroking Wombat's ears with my thumb and forefinger, gently rolling them up and then letting them dangle again.

'Saturday,' said Dad. He cut himself a lopsided slice of bread and reaching for the marge he added, 'the day after tomorrow.'

7

I could smell the barbecue from my room. I had the window open because it was hot and the curtains were blowing – filling up like sails. Charcoal and roasting meat and onions. It was making me feel hungry. I switched off the CD player and looked out across the garden. There were dozens of them, sitting on rugs all over the lawn – my age and older – in T-shirts and shorts and baseball caps. They were sitting in groups – teams it looked like – playing a game that involved spinning round and round fast holding a broom, and then running down the garden carrying a cup of water. There was lots of squealing and laughing and people falling over. One girl got water all over her head She chased after a guy in glasses and tripped him over in the grass.

The light was turning orangey and there were long shadows across the garden. The steeple of the church made a thin black triangle, stretching, like a sword, over the grass.

I could see Dad, standing with a long fork in his hand, poking sausages. He was laughing. He had on an apron that my uncle bought one Christmas that said, 'Old Vicars never die, they just Altar a lot!' Reg Bennett was there too, in an apron with Snoopy wearing a chef's hat on it. Reg Bennett is like Ned Flanders. He runs the kids' activities at our church – Dad's church – and he smiles a lot. So do all his kids. They all wear matching home-knitted jumpers too.

The chicken wire had worked – so far, at least. I had helped Dad build the pile of bricks in the afternoon. Then we'd dragged the roll of wire in from the garage. There's all sorts of junk in there – stuff that's just been dumped. We came across a wheelchair of Mum's, an old heavy thing that she had when she first needed one. At the end she had a hi-tech wheelchair with a head rest and foot rests and arm rests and a special electric cushion to help her circulation. All mod cons, she liked to say.

I was thinking about Mum as I looked out across the grass and suddenly felt a pang of loss, like a sharp stabbing pain. There I was, leaning on the window sill, watching a crowd of strangers cavorting in our garden, with the smell of sausages wafting up to me. It happens like that – suddenly out of nowhere I find myself feeling angry that she's gone, feeling cheated. Or I'll be in the middle of a conversation with someone – about anything – and out of the blue I'll find I'm fighting back tears. You can't explain it and you can't control it either – it's like shivering when a cool breeze passes across you.

Wombat stole the sausages while we were in the garden building the barbecue. We'd left them out on the kitchen bench, defrosting. I found them in Wombat's bed, still frozen rock solid and wrapped in their cellophane – all except for one that was poking out. It had recognizeable teeth marks in it.

'I think we'd better sling that one!' I said.

'Definitely,' Dad said, 'we don't want to poison anybody. Wouldn't the paper just love it? Front page news... Church made me sick!'

We laughed. The papers are always after stories about Dad. They ran a cheesy piece about Mum's funeral – Tragic Vicar Says Goodbye! I had to deliver it through fifty doors.

'Church made me sick!' Dad said again, chuckling to himself. Then he looked at me meaningfully. I could tell he wanted to say something. He went all fidgety and cleared his throat and then he said, 'You're really welcome to come, you know – and join in, tonight. There'll be a lot of people your age...'

I was pretty non-committal. 'Maybe I'll come for the food...' I said, smiling.

I'll have to admit I was curious when they all arrived. I was peering out round the curtains like Mrs Ferguson along the road does – you know, peeping out from behind the nets, the nosy old cow! The garden was filling up with noise. Part of me did want to join in, to be down there, but I felt shy – too shy to go and mingle and meet a load of people I didn't know. And I certainly didn't want to join in with the religious bit. I heard Dad welcome them all, in his church voice, and say a prayer and then I could hear singing. Two guys played guitars and there was a girl playing a flute. A few people were dancing. They sang loudly – songs about God. I didn't know many of them but then our church doesn't really go in for groovy music.

After the singing I heard a shout and a roar of laughter. Then a woman in a pink T-shirt shouted, 'Grub up – and don't kill each other in the rush,' and people started queuing for hot dogs and chicken legs.

I looked in the mirror. I was getting a nice tan but my nose was peeling a bit, all flaky and white. At least the sun had cleared my spots up! I actually looked quite healthy. Maybe even handsome – with a bit of imagination! Clare says I look like Bono. (Early Bono, when he was in his prime!) It must be the big nose. I was wondering if it would be possible to go and get a hot dog without speaking to anyone. The smells were getting too much for me. Maybe I could get something to eat and then slip off again – go and watch telly, or talk to Wombat or something. Wombat was banned from the garden for the evening. He was shut in the kitchen. I could hear him whimpering. Poor Wombat. All those delicious smells and fifty new people to lick and be fussed by. It must be like canine torture, being shut out. I patted him on the way out of the back door and promised to save him a sausage.

The queue was thinning out by the time I got there. Dad winked when he saw me and Reg Bennett beamed so much I thought his face would split. Just as long as he doesn't think it means I'll be back at church!

'Onions?' he said, holding up his ladle. I shook my head. I hate onions on hot dogs – especially when they go all yellow and slimy. I upended a bottle of tomato sauce and squirted a snake of it the length of my sausage. The food was hot through the paper serviette – almost too hot to hold.

I took my hot dog and a cup of orange squash and stood by the hedge, by myself, feeling awkward, concentrating hard on my food. It was odd feeling like a stranger in my own garden. Everyone else seemed to be in groups, talking, as if they knew each other. I felt a bit like an impostor. People would assume that I was one of them – that I was dead religious. Suddenly this girl was speaking to me.

'You must be from the other group,' she said, 'because I don't recognize you...' I looked up from my hot dog. The girl was small and pretty and wearing dungarees that looked as if she'd cut the legs off. I could feel myself blushing.

'No, I'm from here,' I said. I noticed that her blonde hair was all wet and at the edges little wispy bits had dried into spikes round her face.

'Was it you that got water over you?' I said, pointing to her hair.

'Oh yeah,' she said, laughing, 'but it soon dries!' Then she said, 'It must be nice to live at the seaside. Do you live near the beach?'

She was smiling up at me, biting a chicken leg.

'I live *here*,' I said, pointing at the grass, 'I mean, literally, here. This is my garden.' It seemed a bit of an odd thing to say, looking round at all the people.

'Oh I see!' she said. 'So is your dad…?'

'Yes, he's the vicar.' What a conversation stopper, eh? I licked sausage fat off my fingers and wiped my mouth on the serviette. I always worry that I might have tomato ketchup all over my face in situations like that. I felt uncomfortable. I hate telling people my dad's a vicar. Round here, everyone knows anyway. They've already got me labelled, and they've got their ideas about what I should and shouldn't be like.

The girl was laughing – not in a mocking way – but as if she was amused. I wondered what was so funny.

'Don't worry,' she said, 'I know the feeling…'

She was twiddling a wisp of her hair with her little

finger. I looked at her, wondering what she meant and she said, 'I'm a vicar's kid too.'

I don't know why I was so surprised but I was. She didn't look like a vicar's daughter, but then I probably don't look like a vicar s son... but then, why should either of us look any different from anyone else? It was just, I suppose, I'm so used to feeling a bit odd... like I'm one of a kind – the last surviving member of the species – and I've never met other vicar's children before... not my own age, anyway. And not nice-looking like she was...

'I'm Jodie,' she said. I was looking at her with a stupid smile on my face – just staring.

'What's your name?' she said after a moment. I think I went red.

'Oh, sorry,' I said. 'It's Tony.'

'Are you going to be around this week?' Jodie was gnawing the last bit of meat off her chicken bone. In the background someone was playing a guitar again. I looked across the garden. The light was starting to go. I could see the sea beyond the hedge, catching the last orange rays in a thin band on the horizon, like molten metal.

'Well...' I said, hesitating. I wasn't sure how to read the question. Was she asking because she liked me, or just because she was friendly? And did she mean, was I part of the Beach Festival...?

'Well...' I said guardedly, 'it depends what you mean by around...' I scrunched my paper serviette into a ball and tossed it in the air '… I'll be here… but I'm not really involved in the beach thing, well, not at all involved actually… it's not really… well, not really…'

'Your scene?' said Jodie, raising her eyebrows. She had really blue eyes – light blue, like swimming pool water.

'Yeah, I suppose,' I said.

'You might be surprised,' she said. I didn't reply.

'Here, I'll take your rubbish,' she said, reaching out for the ball of paper. She took it and headed off to find a bin. I heard her say, 'Thanks, that was delicious,' to Dad and then Dad said something to her that I couldn't quite hear but I think it was about me because Jodie glanced round at me and grinned.

I suddenly thought of Wombat, in solitary confinement, so I took the last sausage off the blackened grill and headed for the house.

Scrambling down the cliff path with Wombat later on, I could still smell the charcoal smoke and I could hear the sound of singing drifting out of the garden behind me. As I reached the sand the voices all but disappeared, drowned out by the gentle sloshing of the tide against the darkening beach.

'You might be surprised,' I heard Jodie say again. 'We might be surprised, Wombat!' I shouted and we set off at a jog along the cool sand.

8

My bike needed a good clean. I'd upended it in the back garden and was rubbing at the wheel rim with a wet cloth. The chrome bits between the spokes were peppered with rust, in tiny spots that felt rough as you touched them. I'd mixed myself a potion with that white cleanser stuff we've got for cleaning the bath and some vinegar, and I was rubbing it onto the metal.

It was the day after the barbecue, another sunny day. I had my shirt off to let the sun get at my back and I'd put my bike in the sunniest corner of the garden, the bit where there's a triangle of paving between two stone walls. That was always the prettiest bit. Dad used to plant flowers there, in tubs, and there's a honeysuckle running up the wall that gives off a brilliant smell in the evening. Mum liked to sit there in her wheelchair on fine days. It's a bit messy now – more weeds than flowers. There's an old Christmas tree in a plastic pot. Its branches are the colour of rust and they look all dry and powdery as if they'd fall apart if you touched them. We'd all thought it was dead, but as I sat there, rubbing at my bike, out of the corner of my eye I noticed tiny shoots of green – pale and fragile looking. They were poking out of the end of each arm, unfolding into soft needles.

The Christmas tree was something of a sore point. Dad invited Cath to spend Christmas with us. He did ask me first whether I minded or not, but it wasn't as simple as minding or not minding so I just said it was fine. 'Fine' – that word again! Tony Sharp's duck-the-question word.

Grandma was really miffed about Cath. Grandma – that's my mum's mum – had expected to spend Christmas with us too, as it was the first year since Mum died. But that would have been worse – she's so morbid and miserable. It wasn't that I disliked Cath, particularly – she's nice enough to me – it was just something about the way she made herself so at home, the way she spread out, the way she filled up the house with her perfume and her laughter and her music. Dad's suddenly into opera since he met Cath. She sends him CDs through the post and he plays them too loud on the tinny CD player in the kitchen while he's making toast.

We'd never had a real tree before – always an artificial one, the same one as long as I could remember. It's green and silver – tinselly – getting a bit threadbare. It spends the year in the cupboard in the spare bedroom, folded flat in a long, thin box – and we always get it out on the Sunday before Christmas. You have to bend the branches down into place like one of those rubbery toys with wire in their arms that you can move and fix in position. Getting the tree out is always my job – well, was my job, mine and Mum's. She'd sit in the armchair and give me advice and I'd put the decorations on, and the lights and the tinsel. We had this running joke that she was 'Decorations Manager' and I was 'Decorations Technician'.

Dad and Cath bought the one in the pot at the garden centre by the golf course. They were giggling when they came in with it, staggering under its weight.

'Doesn't it smell wonderful?' Cath said as they set it down in the living room. 'I love the scent of pine in the house. There's nothing like it!' Dad was smiling at her like he always smiled at her.

'We got a living one,' she said, 'with roots – so we can put it in the garden after Christmas, and use it again next year…'

'What about the old tree?' I said feebly. Dad wasn't really listening.

'Oh, that old thing,' he said dismissively, 'it's a bit past it…'

It was then I walked out and slammed the door. Dad and Cath didn't understand why. I wasn't sure I understood myself. The tree *was* a bit past its best and the pine one *did* smell nice… but it wasn't that, it wasn't the tree at all. It was Dad. I remember reading at school once that when someone died in Victorian times you wore black for a whole year afterwards – mourning clothes, so that everyone could see your grief. Dad was the complete opposite. He seemed more bright and cheerful now than he ever was *before* Mum died. In fact he seemed really happy, sick-makingly happy. He was moving too fast. Things were changing too quickly. Mum had only been dead nine months – nine months and a week – and this was my first Christmas without her – ever.

I went to my room and played my music loud – loud enough to annoy them – like I always did. I thought that was it – that I'd made my point, but the next day, for no reason at all, I suddenly burst into tears in the middle of lunch. I can't even remember what triggered it but I remember sobbing and saying how much I missed Mum and saying I wanted to do things the way she would have wanted. Cath cuddled me and stroked my hair. That was the first time she ever touched me. I felt embarrassed afterwards, as if I'd acted like a kid.

But they got the old tree out and we had two.

'Past, present and future,' Cath said, 'like Mr Scrooge's ghosts.' She bought me a really nice shirt for Christmas and a painting of a seagull – a little one in a glass clip frame.

'I just saw it in a shop,' she said. 'Your dad told me about Bono. I thought you might like it…'

I put it on the shelf in my bedroom, next to the photo of Mum in a sunhat.

The tree looked dead by New Year. Its leaves were brown and most of the needles were on the carpet.

'So much for being a Living Tree!' Dad said. We stuck it in the garden and forgot about it, but now it was growing again. I wondered if it was a sign of something and then I thought how much like Dad that was – to try to find a message in everything. His sermons are full of things like that – plants and pictures and funny stories that represent some bigger truth. Everything's got a purpose in Dad's world, it all fits together like some big jigsaw.

The rust on my bike wheels was beginning to shift and underneath the metal was shiny. I could see my face in it, all distorted – small and misshapen, with overgrown eyes and an enormous nose. I pulled an ugly face at myself.

There was still a vague smell of charcoal from the barbecue in the garden even though Dad had poured water over the smouldering embers before he went to bed.

'Better not set the house on fire!' he'd said.

I helped him wash up after everyone was gone and Wombat licked the pan where the sausages had been and sniffed hopefully amongst all the crumpled paper serviettes. Neither of us mentioned Jodie but I reckon we probably both wanted to. I kept thinking about her, now, as I polished my bike.

I was thinking about her when I heard a wolf whistle behind me and I looked round, startled, and blushed to find Clare. I felt suddenly guilty, though I wasn't sure why. I had no reason to be. It wasn't as if Clare and I were going out together any more. There was no reason why I shouldn't see someone else. But then I wasn't even seeing Jodie – I was just thinking about her...

'Hi!' Clare said. 'You're getting a very sexy suntan!'

She was wearing shorts and a skimpy white top. She sat down on the grass and started turning the pedals of my bike so that the back wheel spun round making a soft ticking sound.

'It was getting rusty,' I said.

'I'll help,' said Clare. She picked up the rag and dipped it in the smelly white gloop.

'What's that smell?' she said.

'Vinegar,' I said. 'It's Tony's Own Special Rust Remover – I'm thinking of marketing it...'

'No, not that smell... like burning or something...'

'Oh, that,' I said. I was hoping she wouldn't notice. 'It's charcoal. We had a barbecue last night.'

'Thanks for inviting me!' said Clare with a pretend hurt face. That was exactly how I expected her to react. She's so predictable.

'Well, it wasn't really anything to do with me,' I said. 'It was more, Dad – well it was – you know that festival thing – there was that bit in the paper about it...'

Clare interrupted.

'Oh! That lot! I'm glad I wasn't invited then! I've just passed them on the beach, making a racket with guitars and tambourines – Bible bashing! They're supposed to be going to convert us all, aren't they? I reckon I'll stay away from the beach for a while. Were they all weirdos? They looked it. Right bunch of religious nuts...'

Clare was going on and on. She sounded just like her mother. Clare's mum is an atheist – or so she says. She thinks all forms of organized religion are evil. The church is 'an instrument of oppression', she says, 'especially of women'. I hate the way Clare slags things off before she knows anything about them. She always has to have something clever to say about everything... and she always has to be right.

'You should get some of that rust remover that you paint on with a brush,' she said, dropping the cloth on the path, 'this stuff's useless.'

'I didn't ask you to help!' I snapped. I felt dead annoyed with her. She has this way of making me feel small – as though I don't know anything – as though I can't think for myself.

Clare was standing up, brushing dried grass off the seat of her shorts.

'Actually,' she said, 'I came to see if you wanted to go

for a walk…' She narrowed her eyes and looked hard at me.

I wanted her to go away so I made an excuse: 'I'm a bit busy at the moment…' I said.

She could tell there was more to it than that.

'Suit yourself,' she said, tossing her head in a huff. 'I know when I'm not wanted!'

I watched her go and felt sad. Sometimes I almost hate her. That seems an odd thing to say about your best friend, doesn't it? I wondered what Clare would make of Jodie. She probably wouldn't like her because she's pretty. Clare is pretty, too, in her own way. But she's unusual – sort of wild looking. Clare usually thinks pretty girls are frivolous and empty-headed. Jodie didn't seem empty-headed.

Clare didn't look back as she went out of the gate. I threw down the polishing cloth and swore. Wombat appeared and lay down in the grass, scrubbing his back on the dried-out soil, as if he had an itch. I leaned across and scratched him and he flicked his tail appreciatively.

'Women!' I said lying back in the sun. 'I don't understand them, Wombat!' Wombat didn't look bothered. He licked my face and, at the sound of my voice, he wagged his tail a little harder.

9

There was quite a crowd clustered on the soft sand at the base of the cliffs, beside the shuggy boats and the bouncy castle. It was about mid-day and people were queueing at the hot-dog caravan at the bottom of the slope. You could see them from the road at the top. I scrambled down the cliff path onto the sand and, skirting round the crowd, I stood some way off with my back to the sea. There was a cool breeze coming off the waves and the tide was high up the beach. A bunch of kids were swimming, playing with a rubber dinghy – clambering onto it and then rocking it violently so that they all fell into the water.

I could see a stripy tent thing like a Punch and Judy stand and there was some sort of puppet show going on. About a dozen children were sat in the sand watching. I could see their faces. Some were laughing, one looked bewildered and was crying, and another sat staring wide-eyed and transfixed while ice cream ran in rivers down her arms.

Behind the puppet show there was a big spray-painted banner that said 'Life In All Its Fullness'. It was hung between two wooden poles stuck in the sand and it was swaying slightly in the breeze. A dog ran across behind it and cocked its leg on one of the poles.

I hadn't planned to come down to the beach – I had this idea that I might go for a ride on my bike. I'd finished cleaning it – but I felt as if I couldn't keep away. It was as if there was a magnet pulling me. Partly it was curiosity. I wanted to see what was going on – what all the fuss was about. And certainly I wanted to see Jodie. But there was more to it than that. I sort of wanted to spite Clare – to go and watch just because it would annoy her.

The puppet story finished and there was clapping and then two clowns appeared in red noses and orange wigs. Their make-up was damp and streaked with the sun. They were juggling with coloured balls and someone was playing a roll on a drum. I thought about the boy with the black dog on Arran, juggling tennis balls at the mouth of his tent.

'Do you ever feel as if life's like juggling?' shouted one of the clowns.

Two guys in shades with cans of lager and Arnold Schwarzenegger chests stopped to watch.

'No!' shouted one of them in reply. The other yelled

something about keeping his balls in the air and people laughed. In the ice cream queue a row of blank-faced tourists watched as the clowns flipped the balls from hand to hand.

'Sometimes,' the taller clown continued, 'you feel as though life just goes round and round in circles…'

He spun the balls so that they were orbiting his head and rolled his eyes from side to side. The crowd were laughing and a few more people stopped to watch. The Schwarzenegger twins burped and moved off. I wondered what Gary would say if he came past now.

Wombat was sniffing in the caves. I moved a bit nearer and peered over the shoulders of two women in bikinis cradling little kids. I was looking all over for Jodie but she didn't seem to be there. There were a lot of people I recognized from the barbecue. They were all in yellow T-shirts with LIFE written across the front. Some of them were walking round the edges of the crowd, chatting to people and giving out leaflets. A guy in glasses – it looked like the guy who'd poured water over Jodie's head – came up to me with a piece of paper in his hand. I took it without looking at it and stuffed it in the pocket of my shorts.

'Are you from round here?' he said.

'Yeah,' I answered. I didn't want to talk so I called for Wombat before the guy could ask me anything else and set off at a jog onto the hard sand.

Further along the beach the crowds thinned out. Two

men in wet suits were surfing and on the shiny sand that the tide was just leaving, a little girl was digging a castle with a moat. I ran close to the edges of the waves where the water had left fringes of tiny bubbles like lace. Towards the other end of the bay I nearly stood on a beached jellyfish, lying in an untidy pink blob on the sand. A few metres offshore a man was lying on his back, toes to the sky, bobbing on the waves. Beside him a cocker spaniel was swimming, submerged except for its brown head, holding a stick in its jaws that stuck out like two horns.

I stopped for a breather and picked up a piece of driftwood that the tide had left. I hurled it, boomerang like, into the foamy waves and Wombat splashed in after it sending jets of seawater shooting upwards.

At the end of the beach, where the headland juts out in a point that looks like a dragon's head, I stopped and sat on a rock. I was singing to myself – a U2 song off the *Best of 1990–2000* album. There was no one about. Crouched on the rock, I was playing an imaginary guitar and I closed my eyes and crunched up my face pretending I was singing into a microphone, like I do in the bath. I can't really sing at all. I wish I could. A tiny crab scuttled across a rock beside my feet and disappeared into a pool.

When I got back to the other end of the bay the clowns had gone and a gang of people in yellow T-shirts were singing. The girl on the flute was there again, standing with her back to the ice cream hut. The crowd was dispersing and people were drifting back to their beach towels and picnics. Overhead a few clouds were blowing in from over the sea and the blueness of the sky looked as though it was being gradually diluted.

I bought an orange ice lolly and sat in the sand beside the mouth of the caves. Wombat looked tired and hot. He lay in the shadow of a rock with his chin on his paws.

Suddenly I spotted Jodie. She was talking to an old man with a shiny bald head. He had his trousers rolled up to the knees and his legs were bony and papery pale. Jodie was waving her hands about as she talked, smiling and pointing – at the singers, and the banner, and the steeple of the church high on the cliff top. The man was smiling back and shaking his head. I wondered what they were saying. She looked lovely. Her hair was piled up on top of her head in a bobble thing and it cascaded down one side of her head and swished as she talked. I sucked hard on the lolly so that the tip turned white and broke away, tasteless and cold. Then I sucked the base, catching sticky dribbles as they tried to run down my wrists.

I couldn't take my eyes off Jodie. I kept wondering if I should go and speak to her. It was probably best not to. She looked busy. Anyway she might not remember me – and then I'd look really stupid. The singing came to an end and the yellow people started to pack things away, into big boxes. Someone pulled the wooden poles out of the sand and rolled the banner up like a scroll. Jodie's old man had wandered off clutching a yellow piece of paper. I saw her yawn and stretch and then the guy with glasses – the one who'd given me a leaflet – went up to her and put his arm round her shoulders. The last bit of my ice lolly slipped off the stick and hit the sand before I could catch it.

'Damn!' I said out loud.

I stood up to go, and pulled the creased piece of paper out of my pocket.

'Do you ever wonder what life is all about?' it said on the front. 'Life' was in big letters like on all the T-shirts. I crumpled the paper into a ball and, as I passed the hot-dog stall, I tossed it, and the lolly stick, into the wire rubbish bin.

10

I'd been planning to paint my bedroom for ages. I'd had this idea of painting a mural on the big wall opposite the window and of painting the ceiling to look like sky. I'm not much good at art but Clare helped me draw it on paper a while ago and it looked quite easy. I went into town on the bus to get the paint from a shop near the swimming pool called 'Decor-8'. Clare said to get emulsion.

'It'll be easier to paint with than gloss,' she said, 'less sticky... and easier to get rid of the mistakes!'

Clare reckons she's an expert when it comes to decorating. She and her mum are forever painting their house. They're like a continuous episode of *Changing Rooms*.

I bought white and blue and purple and this brilliant lime green colour that was expensive because it said it would glow in the dark. As I was lugging the carrier bag to the bus stop I spotted a big yellow poster in the window of the Post Office. *Discover LIFE in all its fullness!* it said. On the way home the bus skirted along the cliff top. I saw a flash of yellow T-shirts down on the sand. On the promenade I glimpsed a woman in a wheelchair. A boy about my age was pushing her. For a moment I thought it was Mum... the hair was the same colour. It's strange how often that happens – how often I think I see her.

It took me about an hour to draw in all the lines in rough. I kept making mistakes and doing bits again, rubbing at the pencil marks with a wet sponge. It was a sort of fantasy landscape with big trees and mountains, and on the ceiling I drew clouds – big fluffy ones like candy floss.

The blue paint was paler than I'd intended, so I stirred some of the purple in with it, but that made it go all streaky. I found a big flat brush in the garage with a long handle and I found that if I stood on my desk and stretched a bit I could just about reach the ceiling. I'd done a strip of sky from above the bed to the window when Dad came in.

'Tony!' he said in a voice that made me jump and splash paint down my shorts. 'What are you doing?'

'Isn't that an obvious question?' I said jokingly.

Dad didn't laugh. I'd assumed he wouldn't mind. He's

normally so laid back about stuff like that, and I've got so used to looking after myself that I hardly ever ask Dad's permission to do things.

'Do you mind?' I said. I was suddenly worried. Then I caught sight of myself in the mirror. I had flecks of blue paint all over my hair and face and a big purple splodge on my cheek. I looked at Dad and pulled a sheepish face. He started to smile.

'It's not that I mind...' he said with a sigh. That was a relief! Then he said, 'It's just, well... it seems a bit of a waste... like it's not worth doing...' His voice trailed off.

I didn't understand what he was getting at.

'How d'you mean?' I asked.

'Well... we won't be living in this house forever...' Dad was gazing absent-mindedly out of the window.

'I probably won't want purple trees on my wall forever either, Dad. I just fancied a change. Who's talking about forever?' I said.

Dad wasn't listening any more. It drives me nuts the way he does that – starts conversations and then leaves them unfinished – so that they just peter out. Sometimes he doesn't even finish his sentences.

He came to, blinking, and then he said, 'Well, hadn't you better put some dust sheets down – or you're going to make a heck of a mess.'

Then he was gone. I could hear his feet on the stairs. I looked down at the desk where I was standing. It was spattered with paint in tiny dots, like blue measles. Maybe Dad was right.

It's actually easier with everything covered up. You can paint faster because you don't have to worry about not splashing all the time. I draped some old sheets over all the furniture and Dad helped me take the curtains down. I even swapped my shorts for a dirty white overall Dad gave me. I reckon I looked very professional! I finished the blue – which was most of the ceiling – by lunchtime, and it looked OK. But I had a headache from the smell of the paint and my neck was stiff from looking upwards all the time so I took a break and went for a walk.

It was nice to be out in the fresh air again and Wombat was glad of the walk. There was quite a crowd on the beach – more than the other day. I spotted Jodie when I was only halfway down the slope. She was standing in a line with three other people in yellow T-shirts in front of the banner that had been there the day before, and they seemed to be doing some sort of play. I stopped by the hot dog stall to watch. The guy with glasses was standing on a beer crate shouting through a megaphone and the three people and Jodie were miming and pulling funny faces – jumping about and then freezing like musical statues, or like a series of photographs. Someone else – a girl with orange hair and tie-dyed shorts – was sitting cross-legged in the sand banging a drum. They were acting out a story but I'd missed most of it so I couldn't pick up the thread. It was something about a man with two sons and a king. Jodie was pretending to cry – big silent crocodile tears. She picked up a huge hanky and wrung it out so that drops of water splashed onto the sand. Everyone laughed. I was feeling quite brave so I moved round, along the edge of the crowd, and stood directly in front of her. The sketch finished with the king throwing a party. They all set off party poppers and waved sticks with balloons on the end, and then the five of them stood in a line and took a bow. I caught Jodie's eye and she smiled at me. It was a warm smile – as though she recognized me, as though she was glad I was there.

As I walked away I could feel myself blushing. Jodie disappeared behind the yellow banner and then the two clowns appeared.

'Do you know… life's rather like juggling…' I heard one of them say.

The tide was a long way out and the waves had left grooved patterns in the sand. I walked towards the rocks that stuck out in the middle of the bay and was just stooping to pick up a stone to skim it when I heard her voice behind me.

'Don't rush off,' she said. I turned round and saw Jodie. She looked hot from the drama and her cheeks were all red.

'I was just walking the dog,' I said, trying to look casual, as if I was there by accident.

'What did you think of the show?' she said.

'I didn't really see much of it – just the end. It was good. You were good.' I was smiling at her.

'It's OK. I wasn't fishing for compliments,' she said. Wombat appeared, all wet from diving into the waves. He placed a stick hopefully at my feet and stood there with his jaws open in a doggy grin.

'What's he called?' Jodie asked.

'Wombat,' I said. I picked up the stick and lobbed it out to sea. Wombat ran off and did a belly flop into the waves.

'He's nuts!' I said. I shrugged and laughed nervously. Jodie was looking at my face. I felt self-conscious.

'You're all blue,' she said. I glanced down at my arms. They were freckled with sky blue paint.

'Yeah,' I said, 'I was painting my bedroom.' I couldn't think of anything else to say, so I looked at the sand and for a moment we both said nothing. Then Jodie spoke.

'Well…' she said, 'I'd better get back. We're on again after the clowns. I'll see you…' She said it as though she hoped she would, and I nodded and smiled. I was wishing I wasn't so rubbish with girls – so shy and awkward. I wish I was better at small talk – chat up lines, jokes even.

Wombat came thrashing back up the beach and lay at my feet, gripping the stick as though he wanted me to fight to get it off him. Jodie ran back up the beach and was lost in a sea of yellow shirts. I wanted to go and watch some more but I thought it would look a bit obvious. So instead, I walked the other way, further along the beach. Halfway round the bay I headed towards the cliffs past the beach hire place that stands in the soft sand at the bottom of the steps.

The beach hire place is a big blue hut where you can rent orange deckchairs or little green changing tents or those windbreak things with pointed poles that you stick into the sand. As I passed the window I noticed a scruffy hand-written sign that said *Summer Job Available. Apply Within*. I turned and whistled for Wombat.

11

'It's three pounds fifty an hour, seven pounds a half-day or a tenner for the whole day and they need to leave a tenner's deposit on each item. Chairs they can have for an hour at a time, but tents and windbreaks they've got to have for at least a half day – or it's not worth the hassle for us. Check the stuff as it comes back and then store it in there. Anything that comes back bust put on the other side, and when we get a free minute I'll show you what to do with it. It'll be mostly deckchairs. People don't want the tents any more – not modest like they used to be – they just take their knickers off on the sand in full view of everyone these days! It's all those nudist beaches in Spain that's done it.'

My head was swimming with all the things to remember. 'I'm Lennie,' he'd said, shaking my hand. 'I've worked on Beach Services for thirty-three years. Been here longer than most of the chairs!'

I laughed.

Lennie was short and bald and walked with a bit of a limp. His face had a leathery look as though he'd been outdoors more than most people and he had a tweed cap that looked as if it was permanently welded to his head. He had one of those thick black jackets on – with leathery bits on the shoulders – like bin men wear, and he chain-smoked skinny little cigarettes that he rolled himself.

We had a steady stream of customers all through the first morning. OAPs, mostly, wanting deckchairs. I recognized the old guy with the rolled up trousers that I'd seen Jodie talking to.

'It's mostly the older ones want the chairs,' Lennie said, sucking on his cigarette. 'Young folks just lie on the sand. Twenty years' time they'll all have rheumatism from lying on damp ground – or skin cancer from too much sun!'

I was stacking the orange chairs against the wall of the hut. It was stuffy inside, and dusty too. I could see huge thick cobwebs hanging, like bats, from the wooden rafters.

'Windbreaks is still quite popular,' Lennie continued. 'It's just as bloody windy as it used to be!'

He went into the back room where there was a desk and a wooden chair and an ancient looking camping stove. He sat on the chair and spread out a copy of the Sun on the desk then, turning to the racing page, he took a pencil from behind his ear and started ringing horses' names.

'D'you like racing?' he asked, without looking up.

'Not really,' I said.

I don't really know much about it. When it comes on TV I always turn the sound down because the commentators voices get on my nerves. Lennie was running a grubby fingertip down the column of names.

'Right Little Raver!' he said suddenly. He winked at me as he said it. 'In the two fifty at Doncaster. She sounds like my sort of horse!'

I went outside into the light. A woman with three small kids was dragging a deckchair up the beach towards me. She had a huge bag across her shoulder and a baby in one arm and she was lifting the folded chair awkwardly with the other hand. I went to help her.

'Thanks, pet,' she said, then she turned to the oldest child and snapped, 'I've told you! We haven't any money left. I'll buy you a flipping ice cream when the man gives us the money back!' Man, eh? I was flattered!

I took a crumpled tenner from the till and put it into the woman's free hand. She looked grateful.

It was nearly lunch time. The sky was getting bluer and it was beginning to feel quite warm. At the end of the beach I could see lots of yellow, and a smallish crowd clustered round the bottom of the slope. It was too far away for me to be able to see or hear anything clearly but every now and then I heard music, or laughing or an odd word shouted through a megaphone. I wondered if Jodie was there and what she was doing. I found myself thinking about her a lot and I'd re-run the conversation we'd had beside the rocks so many times in my head that I couldn't remember what she'd really said and what I'd made up. In the reconstructed version I'd already kissed her about three times and she'd said, 'Has anyone ever told you you look like Bono?' Dream on, Tony Sharp! I was pretty sure she liked me, but I'd have to move fast. They were only here for ten days and four had gone by already.

'D'you want some Bovril?' Lennie said, poking his head out of the hut. I went inside. Lennie was boiling up a kettle on the stove, which was giving off a strange gassy smell. Lennie spooned thick dollops of gooey brown stuff into two mugs and poured water on it. It tasted like school gravy. I blew on it so it wouldn't burn my mouth.

'What d'you do in the winter?' I asked Lennie, as he opened a brown paper bag full of sandwiches.

'I work in the botanical gardens – in the greenhouses mostly – just a couple of hours a day, like. And I looks after my missus. She gets arthritus bad in the winter... can't get out much... and she can't cook or 'owt.' He smiled a wrinkly smile at me and added, 'I prefer the summer! Get a bit of peace!'

I noticed a *Sunday Sport* calendar on the wall above the desk. A blonde topless model, with a bikini top hooked over her finger and glossy red lips, was winking at me. I could feel myself blush. I wondered for a moment what Jodie looked like topless, and what it would be like on a nudist beach. Then someone rang the bell by the door and I left my mug of steaming Bovril (thank goodness!) to give three deckchairs to a man with a silver moustache.

'Good heavens! Lennie the Deckchair Man! Does he still work there?' Dad was slouched in a chair in front of the television eating a chicken sandwich.

'Why? Do you know him?' I asked. I'd just had a bath and I was sitting on the sofa wrapped in a big green towel, rubbing at my wet hair.

'I buried his mother about fifteen years ago. He lives in that terrace beside the station – in the end house. He used to work in the park as well…'

'He still does,' I said. Then I said, 'He's nice. He's got this amazing stove that looks as old as him and he wears his coat even when it's roasting!'

Dad laughed.

I went upstairs to put some clothes on. In the bath room we've got a full length mirror on the wall behind the door. I let the towel drop to the floor and looked at myself for a moment. I noticed, looking closely, that I'd grown another hair on my chest – that makes four! My shoulders were peeling slightly from the sun and right in the middle of my back (I could see it if I craned round) there was a big spot – the yellow sort that want squeezing. I tried to reach it but my arms didn't stretch far enough so I combed my hair and pouted at myself a few times. Then I flexed my biceps like Gary. I'm nothing like as muscly as Gary. In fact I looked quite skinny. I thought again about nudist beaches and wondered if I'd ever dare take my clothes off in front of people. Then I pulled on some shorts and went downstairs to watch TV with Dad.

12

It was raining the next day. No one wanted deckchairs. We didn't have a single customer all morning.

'We'll fix some of this lot,' said Lennie pointing to the stack of broken chairs against the wall of the hut. He pulled out one chair with a ripped seat.

'If the material's bust, like this one, we can fix it. All it needs is a new seat. I'll show you in a minute. But if the wood's broken, like this one 'ere...' Lennie yanked out a chair with a frame that was split in three pieces, 'it's not worth bothering. People only complain that the chair doesn't look safe if it's been botched up. Mind, goodness knows how some of them get like this! I reckon some people don't know their own strength. I had one bloke, last summer, couldn't get the thing to open out properly. Reckoned it was jammed or something... snapped the bloody thing in half!' Lennie dropped half an inch of unsmoked cigarette on the wooden floor and ground it to dust with the toe of his shoe.

'If they're beyond repair, sling 'em out the back and the council come and take them away.'

Getting the old seats off was the hardest part. Lennie gave me a thing like a screwdriver with a v-shape in the end of the blade.

'Howkerouter!' he said.

I looked at him blankly, so Lennie explained, 'For howking things out. Howkerouter!'

I laughed.

The key was to wedge it under the tacks along the top of the frame and lever them upwards so that the material was freed from the wood. When it was all off, you had to cut a new length of canvas from a big roll that sat in the corner of the hut and then tack it back onto the frame with a hammer. At first I was all fingers and thumbs and I managed to bash my nail and make it turn purple. It took me over an hour to mend only two.

Lennie was making Bovril again and listening to the racing on a fuzzy little radio propped on his desk.

'How did Right Little Raver do?' I asked.

'Oh, she came in first. Won me a tenner, the little darling,' Lennie said with a chuckle.

'Bovril?' Lennie tilted his head on one side and held the kettle up high.

'No thanks,' I said. I didn't fancy repeating the experience. Most of yesterday's cup had ended up poured on the sand behind the hut, where it had run away in brown rivers.

'You might as well skedaddle for a bit,' Lennie said. 'Doesn't look like there'll be much action for a while.'

The beach was almost deserted. A few people were walking dogs in the edge of the grey waves and a family in raincoats were huddled by the pier eating sandwiches under a big golfing umbrella. One or two old ladies in rubber bathing caps were swimming in the sea. They're there every day – even in winter.

I don't know how they stand it. Maybe they've lost all feeling in their skin after years of swimming in icy water. Most of them are quite fat, like whales – lots of blubber! There wasn't a yellow T-shirt in sight. I wondered what they all did on wet days – where they went, who they found to talk to.

The rain was coming down heavily and I was pretty wet by the time I got up to the top of the cliff and crossed the road. I had a hunch that they might be in the church hall. I'd heard Dad mention that they were using that as their base. It was worth a try, anyway.

The hall is a big wooden building tucked away behind the church in the corner of the graveyard. The lights were on. I'd guessed right. The place was full of people, sitting in groups eating sandwiches and pot noodles. No one noticed me walk in. I stood by the door, glancing round trying to spot Jodie. Then someone came through a door beside me and said, 'Are you looking for someone?'

I panicked and said quickly, 'Er, yes, my dad, er, the vicar... Geoff... have you seen him?'

It was a girl who'd spoken to me – the girl with the orange hair who'd been playing the drum on the beach.

'Has anyone seen Geoff recently?' she said aloud. It seemed odd that she was calling my dad Geoff. I wondered what they all thought of him. People glanced round, and someone said, 'He was here about half an hour ago. Try the house...'

Just then, I saw Jodie. She'd been sitting with her back to me, beside the window, but now she looked round too, and when she saw me she came over.

She had a big chunky sweater on that came down to her knees and her hair was hanging loose right down onto her shoulders.

'Hi,' she said smiling.

'Are you busy?' I felt as though people were watching me. My hair was sopping wet and plastered down on my head. I ran a hand through it to sweep it off my forehead.

'No, we're just killing time, really,' Jodie said. 'Waiting for the Great British Weather to improve!'

'Have you had lunch?' I said. I was surprised that I said it so directly.

'Sort of,' said Jodie. She was looking quizzically at me, as though she was wondering what was coming next.

'It's just,' I said, feeling suddenly embarrassed, 'I was going to get some chips and I wondered if... well... if you might like to come...?'

'I was hoping you'd say that. I'd love to,' she said. I felt a rush of warm pleasure run through me. She was beaming at me just like when I'd seen her on the beach.

When we got outside the rain was coming down like pellets of lead, bouncing off the road and rushing along the gutters in torrents.

'Is it far?' Jodie asked, looking at the sky.

'Not really,' I said, 'but if you wait here I'll go and get an umbrella from home...'

I borrowed Dad's umbrella, his big black one, and I held it over Jodie as we walked along the seafront. I could feel her brushing against me as we walked. We went to Mantini's beside the pier and ordered chips and mugs of hot chocolate. I shook out the umbrella and we sat either side of a Formica table against a fogged-up window.

'It's your original greasy café,' I said, picking a cold chip out of the sugar bowl, 'but it's cheap and the chips are brilliant.' Jodie propped her elbows on the table and rested her chin in her hands.

'How come you're so wet?' she asked. I ran my fingers through my hair again.

'I was at work,' I said. 'I've just started working at Beach Services...'

Jodie scrumpled up her brow as though she couldn't work out what that was, so I said, 'Sounds good, doesn't it! It's just the hut in the middle of the beach that rents out deckchairs and things. Lennie calls it Beach Service – Lennie's my boss. I'm on lunch break – well, unofficially. There weren't many people wanting deckchairs today...'

'I'm not surprised,' said Jodie laughing. She sipped her hot chocolate and stared at the table.

'Chips twice!' a voice shouted from behind the counter. I got up to fetch the chips. I felt nervous as I carried them back to the table. I was worried that I wouldn't be able to think of anything to say and we'd just sit there. And I was worried that Jodie might think I was boring or that my breath smelled or that I had a stupid laugh or something.

The café joins on to a Bingo arcade and as we ate we could hear the droning sound of the caller, talking monotonously through a microphone... 'Two little ducks, twenty-two... Legs eleven... Two fat ladies, eighty-eight... Over the top of the voice came the electronic bleeps of a room full of video games and slot machines.

'What a racket!' Jodie said, shouting above the noise. 'Is it always this busy?'

'Only in summer,' I said. 'Most of the amusements and stuff are closed in winter and the beach is really quiet out of season…' I dipped a chip in a pool of tomato sauce and bit the end off it.

'Have you lived here long?' Jodie asked.

'All my life,' I said. That wasn't strictly true. We lived in Surrey until I was about two, but I couldn't remember it. This was the only place that felt like home. I can't imagine living anywhere else.

'Where d'you live?' I asked, biting into another chip.

'On the Wirral,' she said, 'Near Liverpool.'

'You're not a Liverpool fan, are you?' I said, making a sign of the cross with my fingers, like people do to ward off Dracula!

Jodie laughed.

'No, but my brother is,' she said. Then she said, 'You've met him. He was talking to you on the beach the other day.'

I didn't latch on to what she was saying at first. 'What?' I said. 'The guy with glasses… the one who poured water over you at the barbecue?' Jodie nodded and I started to laugh.

'What's up?' said Jodie, blowing on a chip to cool it down.

'I thought he was your boyfriend,' I said. She blushed and made a funny sort of squealy sound into her chips, then she said, 'No! That's Simon. My big brother!'

To say I felt glad is an understatement. I could feel myself smiling and my cheeks getting warm.

'Have you got brothers and sisters?' Jodie was slurping the last bit of her hot chocolate.

'No,' I said, 'There's just me and Dad.'

She looked at me and narrowed her eyes. 'What about your mum,' she said.

It came as a shock to me that she didn't know. There was no reason why she should – and no way she *could* know – unless someone at church had told her – Reg Bennett, maybe? But all the same, there was something amazing about the fact that here was someone who didn't know all about Tony Sharp's ill mum. About poor Tony Sharp whose mother died… but don't mention it or he might get upset… Here, in front of me, was someone who knew nothing about me at all. I was an unwritten page. I had no past. I was just Now. Tony, with wet hair and a peeling nose.

'She died,' I said. 'Just last year. At Easter.'

Maybe I said it too abruptly – I was thinking more about me, about being unknown, than I was about Mum. Jodie looked horrified.

'I'm sorry,' she said. 'I didn't think… Oh, how awful…' People hate talking about death – you can see them backtracking, trying to swallow what they've said, change tack, change the subject.

'It's OK,' I said. 'She was ill for a long time… always, really… well it seemed like that… but now she's… well, she's gone…' I don't think I finished what I was saying. I was suddenly choked up. Gone. Gone where? Gone how? I rubbed at the misted windows, clearing a porthole to see out onto the wet street, and sending showers of dribbles down the glass.

Jodie had finished her chips. She sat back in her chair and ran her hand through her golden hair. I drank the last drop of my chocolate in silence, then I said, 'I'd better get back to work. It looks as if the rain's easing off.'

When we got to the door, I said, 'Thanks for coming,' and Jodie said quietly, 'Thanks for the chips.'

'I'll walk back with you, so you don't get wet,' I said.

The promenade was awash with puddles. A car shot past us and sprayed my legs with sandy water. Out on the horizon, just above the sea, the bank of cloud had broken and a tiny patch of china blue was pushing its way out. We walked, close together under the black umbrella, and neither of us spoke.

13

There was a cold wind blowing off the sea. We were playing crazy golf. My ball, rolling down the green rubbery tarmac, was caught by a strong gust and blown off course into the concrete bunker.

'Unfair!' I shouted. 'Weather interference!'

Jodie laughed and placed her golf ball carefully on the white spot at the end of the strip. She stood sideways, leaning on her putter, and wobbling her knees like a cartoon golfer.

'Hole in one coming up!' she said and took a swipe at the ball. It shot along the green and hit the wooden slats of the bridge with a thwack.

'Unlucky!' I said with a grin.

We were on hole number six. The tarmac slopes slightly downhill towards a little red bridge with a narrow gap under it and the hole is hidden from view round a slight bend on the other side of the bridge.

'This is the worst of the lot,' I said, 'I've never done it in less than three.'

'How many times have you been round this course?' Jodie asked. She was fishing her ball out of the bunker.

'Hundreds!' I said with a grin.

'You'd never guess,' said Jodie, and she winked at me. I pulled the little blue scorecard out of my pocket. Jodie was winning. She'd got a hole in one at the windmill, which was a sheer fluke. You have to get the ball through a gap in the bottom of the windmill, without hitting the sails as they spin around. Jodie said her success was due to her perfect split-second timing. I said it was beginner's luck.

It was a sunny day and the sky was bright blue. If it hadn't been so windy it would have been quite hot. Jodie wedged her putter between her knees and, holding her pencil in her teeth, pulled a sweatshirt over her head. I shivered a bit. 'It's freezing, isn't it?' I said. My arms had gone all pimply.

'That's why people go to Tenerife!' said Jodie, flicking her hair out of her eyes.

We finished the hole – me in three more shots, Jodie in two – and stopped beside the spot for number seven.

'This one's a doddle,' I said, taking a practice swipe with my putter. The course is split level with the hole down a step from the green.

'The key is to hit it just hard enough so it plops down the step and stops right by the hole,' I said. I sounded like a real pro.

'Sounds a cinch!' said Jodie smiling.

A dad and three small children were in front of us. The smallest child could barely hold the club and he was thrashing about, swiping at the air and failing to make contact with the ball. He had a stubborn look on his face. The oldest child was busy hitting his sister over the head with his putter. The dad looked hassled. He kept glancing up at us, waiting at the start of the green.

'Come on, Alex,' he said, 'we can't take all day over one hole. Just pick it up! These people are waiting to have their turn. Just pick it *up!*' He shouted really loud, as though he'd been bottling it up, and the child burst into tears and bashed his golf club down on the ground.

The dad looked dead embarrassed.

'Don't worry about us,' I said, 'we're not in a hurry!'

It was true. I was in no hurry to finish. Jodie leaned on the fence looking out across the sea. Some people in wet suits were surfing in the white of the waves and the red flag was flying.

'That flag means it's dangerous to swim,' I said pointing to it. 'You get strong currents on this coastline when it's windy. Some kids got washed out to sea last summer on a rubber dinghy.' Jodie's hair was blowing across her face, covering her eyes. She tugged at it with her fingers. I thought how nice she looked. She had the dungarees on that she'd been wearing at the barbecue, and pink baseball boots. I was very glad she'd come.

It was her day off – her one rest day – no drama, no singing on the beach, no chatting to old men. I had her all to myself. Just Tony Sharp and the Promenade Crazy Golf!

'I'll show you the sights of the seaside,' I'd said. I'd gone looking for her in my lunch break yesterday. After the other day at Mantini's I felt much braver about her – as if I'd tested the water a bit and it was OK to get in. She'd called for me at the Vicarage at ten o'clock. Dad did this wink as I came down stairs – a really obvious embarrassing wink. I don't think she saw – thank goodness! I'd spent ages deciding what to wear and I still wasn't ready when the doorbell rang.

Now it was half past eleven. We had the whole afternoon to fill. I was worried that there wouldn't be enough to do, that Jodie would be bored... after the Crazy Golf and the beach and the amusement arcades there's not a fat lot else to see. I glanced sideways at her as she leaned on the railings. She didn't seem bored at the moment.

'Finished!' the man shouted. We looked round. The little boy was smiling and holding his golf ball up proudly.

'Hole in twenty-four!' his dad said with a laugh.

I managed to pot the ball in two but Jodie took a lot longer.

'Experience is telling now,' I said laughing at her. Jodie's ball was only about a foot from the hole. She swiped it too hard and it skated round the edge settling the same distance away on the other side. I smirked and Jodie stuck her tongue out at me and I thought how relaxed I felt with her, considering we hardly knew each other.

Hole number eight is a series of bumps with a great big bunker in the middle of the green, and the last hole is hidden underneath a space rocket – under the tail where the flames would be if it was taking off.

'Thunderbirds are go!' I shouted as I sliced the ball towards the rocket.

'FAB, Brains,' said Jodie.

Jodie was sitting on a patch of grass, totting up the scores. She was biting the end of the pencil and furrowing her brow.

'It's pretty close,' she said.

'Loser buys the ice creams,' I said, flopping onto the grass beside her.

'That's you,' she said. 'Thirty-three, thirty-one.' I snatched the blue card from her. 'You've got to ring the bell now,' I said as we stood up.

'I thought we'd finished,' Jodie said.

'This is the bonus,' I said. 'You have to hit the ball up that ramp so that it goes down the top hole and rings the bell.'

The ramp is on the front of a wooden hut that looks like a hen house. There are three or four holes on either side of the top one, like in pinball.

I went first. I hit my ball too far to the left and it ran down the ramp into one of the side holes.

'Never mind,' said Jodie with mock sympathy.

She placed her ball at the bottom of the ramp and walloped it with the club. It sailed up to the top and popped down the hole. The bell rang loudly and the ball appeared again, out of a trap door at the bottom.

'Now what happens?' said Jodie.

'You can go round again, or you get a free pass for next time,' I said.

We handed our clubs and pencils back to the man in the booth and he gave Jodie a piece of paper with a date stamp across it.

'You can use this any time in the next five years, pet,' the man said.

Jodie folded it carefully and put it in her pocket.

'You'll have to come back specially,' I said, stuffing my hands into the pockets of my jeans. Jodie smiled and said nothing.

We went to Mantini's for the ice creams. It was too blowy to eat them outside. We sat at the same table as before, looking out at the windswept promenade.

'Sometimes when it's stormy,' I said, 'the waves come

right across the road. And when it dies down again there's sand all over the pavement.'

We ordered ninety-nines – double sized ones. Jodie had strawberry sauce all over hers and it ran down onto the cornet in thick pink dribbles.

'Did I upset you the other day?' she said suddenly. We hadn't talked since – not about Mum – so the question came as a surprise. I looked at her over the top of my ice cream.

'When I asked about your mum?' she added. She needn't have said that. I knew what she was on about. I nodded, and bit the top off my flake and said, 'No.' Then I said, 'It was just odd that you didn't know. Sort of weird. I mean, here, everyone knows and people treat me differently – you know, they're careful what they say, and if they come out with something like 'I'm dying for a drink,' they get all embarrassed and start apologizing… well, not so much now, but they did at first. People get so uptight about saying the wrong thing that they don't talk to you at all…'

'Do you mind talking about her?' Jodie asked. She took a mouthful of ice cream and wiped her lip with her finger.

'No, I like talking about her… well, like is the wrong word really. I suppose I need to talk about her… I think about her a lot…' I suddenly felt as if I was going to cry. I swallowed hard and looked out of the window. In the next door room the slot machines were bleeping and the bingo man was barking out his lists of numbers.

'What did she die of?' said Jodie quietly.

'She had MS,' I said. 'She actually died of pneumonia, but it was because of the MS that she got ill.' That made it sound too sudden, like she just got ill and then she died, when in fact she was always ill, she just got worse, so I added, 'She had it for eighteen years.'

We were sitting in our kitchen when I mentioned Clare. I was making cheese on toast. (Jamie Oliver watch out!) Jodie was sitting at the table, stroking Wombat's ears.

'Would she mind you seeing me?' Jodie asked.

I had my back to her, fiddling with slices of toast. I knew fine well that Clare would be hopping mad. She's quite possessive about me even though it's a year since we split up. She'd be especially mad that Jodie was connected with the beach festival.

'She might,' I said, trying to sound off hand, 'but it's ages since we stopped going out together…'

'Do you still see her a lot?'

I lifted a piece of toast off the grill and dropped it quickly, jerking my hand away from the heat.

'She's kind of like my best friend,' I said, sliding the toast onto a plate. I put it on the table in front of Jodie.

'Thanks,' she said. Then she asked, 'Why did you split up?'

I felt annoyed with her. Why did we have to talk about

Clare? Clare was the past and anyway what went on with us was none of Jodie's business – it was secret, special. It's hardly a recipe for romance to spend the whole of your first date talking about your ex-girlfriend.

'What is this, twenty questions?' I said with a brittle laugh.

Jodie looked stung. 'Sorry,' she said. 'Do you mind?'

I did mind. I sat down at the table opposite her and bit into my toast. The cheese stretched out from my mouth like chewing gum.

Jodie looked like she was waiting for me to talk, so I did, in spite of myself.

'Things got too heavy,' I said, not looking at her. 'We saw too much of each other – it all got a bit much. I was still bombed out after Mum died...' I wondered what Jodie would say if I told her Clare had wanted sex and I hadn't.

'She's keeping well away from the beach festival,' I said with a laugh. 'Clare's definitely not into God!' I remembered what Clare had said in the garden the day I was cleaning my bike, about them all being religious nutters – Jesus freaks!

'What about you?' Jodie was looking at me with her wide blue eyes. It was the first time she'd mentioned it, him, God... I'd been half expecting it... after all that was why she was here – on the 'LIFE' thing – to talk about God and about faith. She must be pretty religious to spend her summer holidays camped on a church floor, talking to strangers on the beach. I didn't know what to say. There was too much to explain. Too much I hadn't got my head round. Too much muddle to know what I thought one way or the other. I chewed my toast, and then I said, 'God and I aren't really speaking at the moment.'

Jodie looked like she was about to ask why. I didn't want to talk about it so I said quickly, 'I don't know why. I just haven't really believed in him… since Mum died, I suppose…'

Believed is the wrong word. You have to think about something to know whether you believe in it or not. To say I hadn't thought – that my mind was still numb, that I'd just pulled the shutters down on the whole subject – would be more accurate. I wasn't even angry with God for taking Mum away: I was just indifferent. Deep frozen. I stood up and dumped my empty plate in the sink. Jodie brushed the crumbs off her hands and rubbed her mouth.

'Do you want to see the lighthouse?' I asked.

Jodie nodded. I think she realized I wasn't up for talking about it any more. Wombat was standing by the back door swaying from side to side and thrashing the air with his tail. I clipped on his lead and, pulling on my hoody, I closed the door behind us.

14

After Mum died there was a lot of bashing and crashing. Some workmen from Social Services came and took out all the hoists and gadgets that we'd had installed for Mum – the stairlift and the pulleys above her bed and above the bath. It seemed a bit hasty – like they were destroying the evidence after a crime… getting rid of all the signs, all the clues. Dad said they were short of funds and probably needed the equipment for someone else. Dad's always so reasonable about everything. Sorting out Mum's personal things took longer. We had no stomach for it. It seemed like a betrayal to get rid of her things, as if we'd stopped hoping. As if we were saying she wouldn't be back. It didn't feel as though she'd gone forever, just as if she was away for a while. Eventually Dad went through her wardrobe and put her clothes in a couple of bin bags and took them to Oxfam. That didn't seem so bad. She could always buy new things, after all. It was the little personal things that hurt most – her treasures. Dad put her wedding ring on a ribbon and hung it on the mirror in their room. I put the eagle picture by my bed.

'Mum wanted you to have this,' Dad said one day. He held out her Bible – the one she always kept by her bed, beside the lamp. It was quite tatty, well thumbed with things scribbled on the sides of pages and bookmarks and cards stuffed inside. I held it carefully and turned to the middle – to Isaiah chapter 40, to the words I'd had in mind when I painted the eagle for Mum. The words were underlined in red pen and there was an asterisk in the margin.

I was sitting on my bed. Dad must have left the room – I didn't notice him go. I must have sat there for ages until I realized the page was damp with my tears. The words were spinning round and round in my head, circling like a bird in flight.

'Those who hope in the Lord will renew their strength… they will soar on wings like eagles…'

When you've been brought up by parents who have based their lives around God – the idea of God, that he is there, and loving and knowable – it's hard to imagine a universe with no God in it. Clare says if there is a God then he's doing a crappy job at running things.

Before Mum died – in the last week when she was

really suffering, when her skin was burning up and she couldn't breathe and they had to tip her upside down to drain the snot out of her lungs – I hated God. If I'd met him face to face I would have punched him. But afterwards, when the silence came, I didn't feel anything. I didn't care whether God was there or not, whether he was nice or whether he was a bastard. It seemed irrelevant either way.

I heard Cath say recently that getting through the funeral is the first hurdle when someone is bereaved, that the real grieving starts after that. Mum's funeral was a sham. I hated it. The church was packed out, fuller than I've ever seen it and when we walked in – me and Dad and Grandma – everyone stood up. We walked to the front and sat on the front row and Dad climbed up into the pulpit. I could feel everyone's eyes on the back of my head, boring into me, like I was a rat being dissected. Mum's coffin was there already – it had lain in the church all morning. It was very tidy – polished wood with shiny handles and covered in pink flowers. It seemed unreal that Mum was inside, that she was in a box with a lid on, all tarted up with flowers like a wedding cake. I had to suppress an urge to jump out of my seat and wrench the lid off the coffin just to check it was her – not someone else's mum. Except it wasn't her – not all of her – not the real part, the part that laughed and cried. The part that loved me.

The funeral was on a Wednesday. She'd died on Friday. Wednesday was the earliest we could get because it was the Easter Bank holiday weekend so Mum was laid out at the Chapel of Rest for nearly a week. Dad and Grandma went to see her every night she was there. Dad said he just wanted to sit with her, and say his goodbyes. I didn't go. Not because I was squeamish about seeing her but more because I didn't really think it was her. The moment she died she was gone. The body lying on the bed wasn't my mum. She was already somewhere else. Someone once told me that dead people don't look real and they were right. How can someone be living one minute and then the next minute not? They must go on living somewhere else. None of it made any sense to me...

It was only when Dad gave me Mum's Bible and I thought about eagles' wings that I knew where she was, and I thought of Bono, circling over the sea – free at last. That was where she was. Somewhere on an eagle's back.

After the funeral there was a party at the Vicarage. Lots of polite ladies from church swept in with plates of scones and salmon sandwiches and endless cups of tea. It was unbearable. Everyone was talking about how brave Dad had been to conduct the service without cracking up – without letting the side down – and they were talking about Mum as though she were a problem removed. 'It

was a blessed release... at least she's not in pain now...'
Such bollocks, all of it!

I didn't stick around longer than I had to. I sat upstairs listening to U2 tapes, drowning out the chink of china and all their stupid empty words. I kept expecting someone to come up and tell me to turn the music down, to tell me I had no respect for the dead, that I was typical of the younger generation who had no sense of occasion – no sense of duty.

I had said my goodbye to Mum in the hospital the Sunday before she died, the day she gave me back the eagle. I'd said it when she could still smile and cry and hold my hand. When she was still real.

15

Cath arrived at the weekend the day after I'd played crazy golf with Jodie. She arrived quite late at night and Dad went to the station to collect her. She hadn't been for a while – not since March or April – I couldn't remember exactly. Dad said things had been busy for her in the parish and she hadn't been able to get away. She brought me a Terry's Chocolate Orange, and she brought a bushy plant that Dad put on top of the television. Dad seemed pleased to see her.

'Geoff tells me you're a working man,' she said to me. 'I'll have to come and hire a deckchair from you. Do you do cut rates for friends?'

I smiled.

'You're looking well,' she said and she winked at me as though there was some hidden meaning in what she said. I wondered if Dad had told her about Jodie. What was there to tell? That I'd been round the crazy golf with a vicar's daughter and been to Mantini's twice! Big deal! It was August already. She'd be gone in a couple of days. I hadn't even kissed her yet. Meet Tony Sharp – fast mover!

I got up late the next morning but I wasn't due at work until after lunch. There was a lovely smell of coffee in the kitchen. Cath had bought Dad an espresso machine for Christmas but we always forget to use it when she isn't here. Wombat was looking like he wanted a walk. He was hopping about with his ears standing on end, head-butting the back door, and tugging at his lead as it hung on its hook by the coats.

I couldn't find my trainers. I hate not being able to find things. I searched all over my bedroom for them, then I remembered I'd kicked them off the night before while I was watching telly. I opened the door to the living room without thinking. The house was quiet so I'd assumed they were out. They were lying on the sofa, kissing each other. Cath's shoes had fallen to the floor and the hearth rug was all rucked up.

I stood motionless, too embarrassed to speak, feeling myself going bright red. I could see my shoes, in the corner by a pile of magazines but instead of getting them, I shut the door quickly and went back out into the hall. Dad must have heard the door because he called out, 'Tony.'

I pretended not to hear but Dad called out again, 'Tony, in here, in the living room,' so I popped my head round the door and said as casually as I could manage, 'Oh, hi! There you are. Have you seen my trainers?'

Dad was standing in the middle of the room looking a bit sheepish. Cath was sitting up, her feet coiled underneath her on the sofa, running a hand through her cropped hair. She smiled a broad smile at me. I picked up my shoes, muttered something about Wombat, and hurried out of the room.

Clare was sunbathing, stretched out on a sun lounger in the back garden. Her sister Kate was there, too – home from college for the holidays. They both had bikinis on and their legs were all shiny with sun oil. There was a radio on the path beside them and they had drinks in tall glasses with curly straws in. Marley, Clare's dog, barked when he saw Wombat and rushed over to sniff at him, his tail pointing straight up like a periscope.

Clare looked pleased to see me. 'D'you want a drink?' she said.

'No thanks,' I said. I didn't want to make small talk with Kate there because she makes me feel about ten years old, and, anyway, I was feeling all churned up – nervous and edgy.

'I was just going for a walk,' I said, trying to sound offhand.

'I'll come with you,' Clare said and, whistling for Marley, she pulled a big shirt over her bare shoulders and pushed her feet into a pair of sandals.

We went to the park. The boating lake was crowded with people rowing little wooden boats and kids going round and round in circles in orange paddle crafts. Along the edge of the water children were trailing fishing nets on bamboo canes and tiny fish wriggled in jam jars like fat tadpoles.

'What's up?' Clare said as we were walking past the swings.

She can always tell when I'm worrying about something – as if she's fitted with some sort of radar system. She says I've got a transparent face. She can tell when I'm lying, too. I shrugged. I couldn't quite put into words what I was feeling – couldn't put my finger on what was bothering me.

'Well, give me a clue,' said Clare, 'is it your mum?'

We sat down on a bench beside the lake.

'Sort of,' I said, scrumpling up my face. 'Well, it's Dad… and Cath… this is going to sound really stupid… I walked in this morning and they were snogging on the sofa like they were our age or something.'

I looked at Clare. She was smiling but she said nothing. So I continued, 'It's partly their age – I mean it's just so odd when it's your dad. I was so bloody embarrassed, walking in on them! But it's Mum too. I don't know what she would think about it… whether she'd mind…'

Clare interrupted, 'Is he happy? With Cath? Does she make him happy?'

I thought of them for a minute – the way Dad looks at her, and all the phone calls late at night, crouched in the hallway, laughing and telling her things. Yes, he was definitely happy – happier than I'd ever seen him. I nodded.

'Well… your mum would have wanted that, Tony… heavens, he deserves a bit of fun after all this time…'

'It's not that,' I said. I kicked a stone with my toe and it rolled into the lake with a soft plop. 'It's just… I don't know… he seems to have got over it a bit quickly. Her dying and everything…' I remembered as I said it how angry I'd been before Mum died, when it had seemed like Dad was almost willing it to happen – like he was resigned to losing her, like he didn't feel anything any more. But then he'd broken down when it happened – when she actually died – he'd cried and cried at the hospital, hunched beside the bed, howling like a little kid. I was really shocked to see him like that. It made me like him more, I reckon.

Clare put her hand on my arm. 'Maybe he just had longer to get used to the idea than you – like he was better prepared or something. She was ill such a long time… it wasn't as if it was sudden…'

I could feel tears welling up, pricking at my eyeballs.

Sometimes I wonder if the tears will ever go away. Will they eventually dry up? Are there a certain number – so many millilitres and one day they'll all have run out? I rubbed my eyes quickly with the back of my hand and shouted for Wombat. Clare squeezed my hand and I smiled a bit pathetically at her. Why does being with her make me feel so safe? I almost told her about Jodie but now didn't seem the time. This was our place, this bench by the lake. As we walked towards the seafront she slipped her arm through mine. I was glad she was there.

'Thanks for coming,' I said quietly.

Clare's house is on the opposite side of the bay from ours. I walked back along the cliff path alone. It was lunchtime and a sudden smell of fish and chips from a shop on the seafront made me feel dead hungry. I rummaged in my pockets to see if I had any cash and found a pound coin and some coppers. I could get some chips nearer home, from the little stall beside the crazy golf.

As I waited in the queue I scanned the beach for yellow T-shirts. There were a lot of people down on the sand – it would be busy at work. There was a long line of people at the hot-dog stand and both the ice cream huts were open. I couldn't see any sign of Jodie and the others. Maybe I'd got the days wrong and they'd gone. A wave of disappointment ran over me like a cold draught. It was only as I walked further round the bay, level with the rocks that stood out at low tide, that I spotted them. They'd moved site, halfway up the cliff to a flat patch of grass, bordered with windswept flowerbeds, just underneath the promenade. The poles of the big yellow banner were stuck into the sandy grass with the back of the banner to the sea, so that you could read what it said from the road, 'Life In All Its Fullness'. I thought of Jodie with her big wide smile.

People were standing on the pavement on the clifftop, watching what was going on. The two clowns were there and one of them was just finishing the juggling routine. I'd never stayed long enough to see the end.

'What you need,' said the clown, flipping the balls high in the air, 'is a complete and utter CHANGE!' As he said the word 'change' he threw two of the balls so that they crossed over each other in mid air.

People were clapping and then some people in black lycra with their faces painted white like Marcel Marceau started doing a sort of mime thing while someone played a saxophone. Over the top of the music a girl was speaking words that were like a poem. I leaned against a bus shelter on the seafront.

'There is a time for everything…' the girl said. 'A time to plant and a time to uproot…' The white-faced figures mimed planting and tearing and then one of them fell on the ground. The saxophone wailed its sad song and all along the promenade I noticed people turning their heads to see where the music was coming from.

'A time to weep and a time to laugh…' said the girl. 'A time to mourn and a time to dance…'

I dropped my chip paper into a rubbish bin and looked hard at the crowd to see if Jodie was there. I couldn't see her. It was nearly one – I was due at work. Wombat was lying on the pavement, panting with the heat.

One of the white-faced figures was hoisted shoulder high by the other three and then they lowered her, face downwards, onto the grass with her arms stretched wide.

'For everything a time and a season under heaven,' said the narrator. 'A time to be born and a time to die…'

I could just hear the last strains of the saxophone tune as I jumped over the vicarage wall.

16

Cath had cooked a special meal – chicken in a sauce with mushrooms and tomatoes in it and new potatoes, and melon for starters. I should have guessed it was building up to something. There were flowers on the table and a bottle of wine. I was tired from work and my shoulders ached from lifting things all afternoon. Inside my shirt, my peeling sunburn was itching and I was sliding from side to side, rubbing my back on the wooden slats of the chair to try and soothe it. The wine was making my eyes feel fuzzy and filling me with a cosy warmth.

Dad was leaning back in his chair. He'd caught the sun on his face and he looked dark and swarthy – almost handsome. He's got grey hair like wire wool – like a brillo pad – and round the edges of his face it's flecked with white. Just lately some of the hairs on his arms have turned white too. Maybe it's the sun.

'That was delicious,' he said, spreading his hands on the tablecloth.

Cath brought the pudding. It was a meringue thing with strawberries on the top and big dollops of cream. I had two helpings and felt stuffed – so stuffed that the waist of my jeans was cutting into my stomach and as I flopped back in my chair I had to hook my thumbs inside my belt to loosen the pressure. Cath was looking at Dad as though she was waiting for him to say something. He took a swig of wine and set his glass down very deliberately on the table. He coughed and cleared his throat and then he said, 'Cath and I have got something we want to tell you...'

I stared at the tablecloth in front of me. There were five little red dots on the white cotton where I'd splashed some of my sauce and it had landed in a pattern like spots on a dice.

Dad sounded tense. 'Over the past few months,' he said, 'as we've talked, and spent time together, and written to each other...'

It sounded like an introduction to one of his sermons.

Dad went on, with a serious look on his face, '...We've had an increasing sense that we enjoy each other's company, and that we're good for each other...'

Just get on with it, Dad! I wanted to say. He fiddled with the end of his spoon.

'And so...' He took an audible breath and smiled

nervously at Cath, '… we've decided that we'd like to get married.'

I was relieved that he'd finally got it out. More relieved than shocked, I think. I suppose I'd seen it coming, especially after what Clare said.

'Congratulations,' I said. It seemed an odd thing to say to your dad. I smiled, first at Dad and then at Cath.

Dad was speaking again. 'It'll mean moving, though, and obviously we want you to feel…'

I didn't hear any more of what Dad said. The word 'moving' hit me like a blow in the stomach and suddenly my mind was spinning with pictures – confused pictures of places I know, and strange nameless faces, and Clare, and Gary and Jodie…

'Where to?' I said bringing myself back to the conversation. I said it more loudly than was necessary.

'Well… we've spoken to the bishop… and it's a case of finding somewhere… a parish…'

I wanted Dad to get to the point. I wanted to know where we were going and when and whether I had any choice in the matter. I wanted to shout, but instead I waited in silence, fiddling with the edge of the tablecloth.

Cath interrupted, 'We're hoping we can find a parish where we can both work, alongside each other, as partners,' she said. Then she added, 'There's a possible place in Nottingham. The vicar's leaving in September and…'

Again, my mind raced off and I stopped listening to

what Cath was saying. Where was Nottingham? I knew the name. It had two football teams – Nottingham Forest and Notts County – I knew that much. But what was it like? Who lived there? How far was the sea? Would there be seagulls? And would it be easier to get to Liverpool, and Jodie?

Cath was looking sympathetically at me. I suppose she knows all about this from her counselling stuff. The impact of remarriage on stepchildren! Fear of change in bereaved teenagers! I was probably reacting exactly as she'd expected. A textbook case!

The room was growing dark as the sun went down and in the half light, her earrings – two big dangling pearls, like teardrops – seemed to glow.

'How do you feel about that?' she was saying, in a soft voice. I felt as if someone had hit me over the head with a brick. I wasn't sure if it was the wine, or being tired, or the shock of what they'd just said.

'Fine,' I said blankly. What else could I say?

I offered to do the washing up but they said something about leaving it till the morning so I excused myself, by saying I was really tired, and went upstairs to my room.

I didn't switch the light on. I lay on my bed, looking at the ceiling. The white clouds I'd painted stood out against the blue and I noticed that the green trees *were* luminous, just as the paint had promised on the side of the tin. In the shadows of the room the colours seemed to throb. I remembered what Dad had said when I was painting the room – about it not being worth doing. Now I understood. It made sense. Dad must have known then that we'd be moving soon. I wondered how long they'd been thinking about it. When had Dad asked Cath to marry him? Or didn't it happen like that at their age?

Wombat pushed the door open with his nose and came and lay across my legs. His tail thumped the bed, making a deep hollow in the duvet. I was thinking about our house, walking round it in my head, into all the rooms – my bedroom, and the kitchen, and the room with the washing machine where we kept Bono. I couldn't imagine living anywhere else. Then I thought of the garden. There's a square in the corner by the hedge that was my patch when I was little. I can remember Dad showing me how to use the hoe, and planting straggly marigolds and nasturtiums that got eaten by caterpillars. I suddenly felt as though I was there – aged six or seven – poking at the soil with grubby hands, and Dad was mowing the grass with the big petrol mower and Mum was lying on a sunbed beside the tubs of lavender. And I was running to her and showing her things I'd found – beetles and worms, and daisies that I'd picked in the grass – chattering to her and making her smile. She had a remission one summer when I was small and could walk again – just for a few months. I can remember it very dimly – or at least I think I can. It's hard to know how much is real memory and how much is a scene you've constructed from all the bits people have told you. I have a picture, in my head, of me clutching on to her hand, walking really slowly along the promenade.

I thought about my patch of garden again. Dad grew rhubarb in it eventually, when I'd lost interest in growing things. I hate rhubarb. I hate the way it makes your teeth go all furry.

I dug my fingers into Wombat's fur and scratched his back. Wombat flicked his tail and made a soft high whimpering noise. I could feel myself sinking into sleep. I dragged myself off the bed and walked to the bathroom. Downstairs I could hear the clink of glasses in the kitchen and I could hear their voices and the sound of Cath laughing.

17

I had to be at work at nine the next day. It was quiet for the first hour, so I sat on the steps in the sun, mending broken deckchairs. I was getting quite expert at it now. I timed myself as I did it with the watch I use when I'm running. My record is twelve minutes and forty six seconds from start to finish. It's straightforward provided the tacks aren't rusty. If they snap on the way out you have to pull the ends out with pliers and that's a bit more tricky. Lennie was in the back room, rolling cigarettes and listening to Radio 2. He looked lost in thought and he was humming to himself as he rocked back in his chair.

I kept thinking about Dad and Cath and what they'd said last night. Why couldn't they get married and stay where they were? Stay where *we* are? Surely that wasn't impossible. Cath could come and live with us here... Dad was always saying how there was too much work in our parish for one person.

I looked along the length of pale sand towards the caves in the headland. The bay was beginning to fill up with people – patches of colour and movement, spreading out from the bottom of the slope. This beach, the sea, the dragon rocks – all of it – seemed to me, as I looked, as though they were a part of me. As if I wouldn't quite be myself if I lived somewhere else. I would be someone else. I would change.

I wondered what Clare would say about me moving. Would she miss me? She's staying on in the sixth-form to do languages – French and German, and English – then we'll probably go to university. Would she keep in touch or would we just drift apart? And Gary – well we've grown apart anyway but I'd still miss him. He's still my mate.

The sun was warming up by the time I'd mended five deckchairs. It had rained earlier on and the sky had been whitish and opaque when I arrived at the hut, but the clouds were shifting now and the sky and the sea were turning a deeper blue. A customer came to hire a windbreak for the morning.

'It looks promising,' he said, raising his palm to the sky. 'The weather man said it would get hotter later on.' He took the green and white striped bundle off to the deep sand at the base of the cliffs and I could see him stretching it out and bashing the poles into the sand with a rock.

Jodie came by at lunchtime.

'Mantini's one more time?' she said. It was her last day tomorrow. She was going back to Liverpool, back to her family and then they were all going off to Wales, camping. She said they went every year. They had one of those big frame tents and canoes and bikes and a Land Rover. I liked the sound of it. It must be cool to be part of a big family.

Mantini's was crowded and two middle-aged women were sitting at our usual table, the one by the window. One of the women was clutching an enormous pink teddy bear in a polythene bag.

'Looks like she's had a win on the Bingo,' I said.

Jodie grinned.

There were two spaces by the counter, so we sat down on high stools, facing a long mirror. I turned sideways so that I didn't have to look at myself all the time. Jodie noticed and laughed.

'Ugh!' she said, 'I don't especially like looking at myself, either. It's enough to put you off your lunch!'

I disagreed. Jodie was looking lovely. I almost said so, but then I stopped myself because I didn't want to sound cheesy. Instead, I just laughed.

Jodie ordered a tuna and salad sandwich. 'I've eaten

enough chips this past week to last me all summer,' she said, pulling a face. I quite fancied chips but I didn't want her to think I was a slob so I ordered a cheese and pickle toastie with coleslaw.

'Have you had a good week?' I asked her as we were waiting for the food. She nodded and smiled, then she flicked her head, tossing her hair out of her face.

'Has it... the thing... the drama and stuff... has it gone OK?'

I wasn't quite sure whether that was the right thing to ask. I wasn't even very sure why they were here. I remembered what Clare had said about them wanting to convert everybody and I wondered if they'd succeeded. It didn't seem very likely, judging by how few people come to Dad's church.

Jodie took a sip of her milkshake. 'It's been good,' she said. 'I've had lots of good conversations with people, especially people our age. People always seem surprised when you say that God likes them...'

'Does he?' I said doubtfully, poking at a pile of coleslaw with a fork. I hadn't really wanted to talk about God. Jodie didn't answer me. She went on saying what she wanted to say, what she'd been planning to say before I interrupted.

'It seems that people either don't think about God at all or they think he's some control freak up in the sky who gets annoyed whenever they start enjoying themselves...' How, I wondered, did she come to be so sure that God was nice? Maybe it's easier to believe that if you've got two parents and a happy life and everything always goes OK for you... I said nothing. When our sandwiches arrived, I changed the subject.

'We might be moving,' I said. 'My dad's going to get married again.'

'That's great!' said Jodie with a huge smile.

I shrugged. 'Yeah,' I said quietly, 'yeah, I suppose it is.'

'You don't look very convinced,' said Jodie. 'Don't you like her or something?'

'It's not that,' I said, 'it's the moving... all the changes...'

I bit into my sandwich, and then, through a mouthful of stringy cheese, I said, 'I've always lived here. This is my place. I can't imagine moving...'

Jodie was nibbling a piece of tomato that had fallen out of her sandwich.

'Moving's OK,' she said. 'We've moved quite a lot. I quite like new places... you'll be all right...'

She stretched her hand out and put it on my arm. It was the first time she'd touched me. I could feel myself blushing. She kept it there a moment and then she dropped it down by her side awkwardly as though she wasn't sure what to do next. I smiled at her and wondered what she'd say if I kissed her. She was talking again, to deflect her embarrassment.

'The house we live in at the moment is huge – even

bigger than yours,' she said, biting her sandwich. Then she added, 'You and your dad must rattle around inside a house that size.'

I laughed. It is a bit ridiculous. Our vicarage is a Victorian place, on three floors, with huge high ceilings – built of blackened stone with dozens of chimney pots. God knows why they used to build vicars such enormous houses. There are loads of rooms we never use, and it never feels very warm.

'Ours is always full of people,' Jodie said, 'so it doesn't seem big. Mum and Dad keep the attic rooms as spare and we often have people living with us...'

'What, you mean lodgers?' I said, licking my fingers.

'Kind of,' said Jodie. 'Usually people with problems who need time to sort themselves out.'

I've got problems, I thought. I wonder if they'd have me! Jodie slurped the last bit of her milkshake. It made a gurgling, plughole sort of noise.

'Once we had this guy who'd tried to kill himself,' she said, 'and once, when I was a kid, we had this woman staying who used to scream in the night – she was pretty screwed up...'

I stared at her. 'Didn't it scare you?' I said.

Jodie fiddled with her hair. 'Yeah, it did a bit,' she said. 'I didn't really understand what was wrong with her at the time.'

'What *was* wrong with her?' I asked.

'She'd seen her dad kill her mum when she was little… and I think he'd sexually abused her as well, her dad I mean.'

'I thought *my* life was complicated!' I said. 'What happened to her?'

'She was all right in the end,' Jodie said, tossing her head back. 'We still see her. She's fairly normal now… and she's got kids. Mum and Dad spent a lot of time with her – sort of going back over bad memories and things and praying… they do that sort of thing a lot… they call it inner healing… people change…'

'Are they nice?' I said. 'Your mum and dad, I mean?' I was trying to picture them. I wondered if they were like Cath. And did they have big eyes like Jodie?

'They're brilliant,' said Jodie with a grin. Then she said, 'You'll have to meet them sometime.'

She looked away, staring at her plate.

'Where's Nottingham?' I asked, wiping my hands on my paper serviette.

Jodie furrowed her brow and twisted her mouth from side to side, thinking. Her face is like rubber – it's always moving!

'Sort of in the Midlands somewhere, I think…' she said vaguely.

'Is it near Liverpool?'

My heart started to beat fast as I said it and I wondered if she could hear it thumping.

She fixed me with her wide blue eyes and said, 'Well…
it's nearer than here.' I gulped hard. How come romantic
moments always make your throat seize up?

'Can we keep in touch?' I said.

Jodie nodded. 'I'll write my address down for you,' she
said. She reached for a paper napkin and wrote her
address on it. 'And that's my mobile number,' she said as
she slid the napkin across the table towards me.

I took it from her and slipped it into my pocket. Then,
swallowing hard, I leaned over and kissed the top of her
head. Her hair smelt of coconut. For a brief blissful
moment we sat still not saying anything, then I noticed
the time.

'Shit! I'd better get back to work,' I said, and I jumped
down off the stool. I did it in such a hurry that I bashed
my leg and fell sideways, knocking the stool over and
losing my balance. In a split second Jodie grabbed hold of
my arm.

'Ooops!' I said and we both collapsed into giggles.

Jodie kept hold of my arm as we staggered out of the
café. The sun was bright outside and I could see it
spangling on the sea. As we headed down towards the bay
I slipped my arm around Jodie's shoulder and I felt a
feeling go through me that was like a warm, comfortable
sigh.

18

The wind was coming off the sea, whipping the waves into white peaks, like meringue. I pedalled hard, thrusting my head down and leaning my weight towards the cliff to offset the wind's effect on my bike. A pale sun was glimmering on the lighthouse, making it look like a ghostly finger pointing to the sky. With clouds racing past it, and swirling overhead, the whole lighthouse seemed to be swaying.

I leaned my bike against the broken fence that edges the most dangerous part of the clifftop path and slithered a few yards down the grassy bank to sit against a rock that was more sheltered. I was high up above the bay, looking out to sea – to Norway, or Holland or wherever it is, way out beyond the expanse of foam. The tide was right in, bashing the bottom of the cliffs. When I was little I used to think that if the tide was in here, it must be out on the other side of the sea, as though the whole ocean just sloshed sideways a bit, like tilting a tank.

I pulled the sleeves of my hoody down over my hands and blew on my knuckles. A drop of rain bounced off my cheek. Out beyond the piers, I could see a fishing boat heading for the mouth of the river, moving slowly, a cloud of seagulls following in its wake. I could see the caves, down underneath where I was sitting – dark holes in the side of the cliff. The tide had reached up almost into them and was sloshing over the slimy stones that litter their mouths like broken teeth. I could see the spot where I'd first seen Bono. I'd presumed he was dead, he was lying so awkwardly, but then when I'd poked him with my shoe he'd squawked and tried to move his wings. I wonder if he's still alive. Seagulls don't live forever, I suppose, and I reckon he was a good age when we first found him.

Overhead a lone gull shrieked and I felt another spot of rain. I scrambled back up the bank and, pushing my bike for a while, I made my way higher onto the headland.

From the rocks above the lighthouse you can see the coastline in both directions. To the North towards home, I could see the familiar stretch of beach. There was Lennie's beach hut, and the ice cream shack – still boarded up from the night – and the church steeple set back from the road. The other way I could see the wide river mouth, and a sandy beach on the south side and, closer to where I was standing, the stretch of dunes where I'd gone with Clare…

'For everything a time and a season under heaven…'
The words of the poem were going through my mind.
Where had Jodie said they were from? Somewhere in the
Old Testament. Ecclesiastes? Was that how you spelt it?

I dragged my bike across a lumpy patch of grass
towards the road. Once I reached the tarmac I cycled fast.
I was thinking about Gary. Gary's working now –
plastering. 'Getting plastered!' he said when I met him in
the street a few days ago. He'll probably stay round here
– get a house near his mum and dad's – marry Sharon,
maybe – and have kids. Little Garys!

What a thought! My own future is a bit more of a
mystery. Everything's changing, shifting – like the sand
under the waves, moving, making new patterns.

I slept badly last night. I had an odd dream – a bit like a
dream I had when Mum died. There was an eagle, flying
over a lake – or was it the sea? It was water anyway – lots
of it, still and very blue. Someone was riding on the
eagle's back but I couldn't see who, and behind, trailing
from the bird's tail feathers was a white sheet, like a
shroud, billowing out like a sail. I was clutching at it,
gripping it tight with white knuckles. And I was riding on
the air currents, borne up by the wind, like paragliding or
something, holding the sheet like the tail of a kite. I could
see the eagle's feathers and the pointed fingerlike tips of

its wings and it was shrieking – a raucous, piercing cry, more like a gull than an eagle.

Below us I could see trees, and rocks and sand – and a group of people staring up at me. Suddenly I felt rain on my face – really heavy rain, soaking me, and then I heard a terrible ripping sound. The sheet was tearing and the corner I was holding was coming away in my hand. Then the eagle was gone and I could feel myself falling, plunging down towards the lake, still grasping the portion of torn cloth in my hands. The rain had stopped and there was bright sunshine, glancing off the water. As I fell, I could make out some of the faces of the people watching from the edge of the lake. There was Jodie and Clare and Dad and Cath, and a man I didn't recognize with a kind face standing behind them. I woke up confused, with the sensation of falling still with me.

I hadn't been into the church since Mum's funeral.

I got the key from Dad's study. It's an enormous iron thing, bigger than my hand. As a child I pretended it was the key to a giant's house. It unlocks the huge wooden doors at the back of the church.

I locked the doors again from the inside so that no one would disturb me. My feet were muddy from scrambling up the cliff path. I rubbed them on the big coconut mat in the doorway. There were no lights on but the sun, extra bright after the rain – as though the sky had been polished clean – was flooding through the leaded windows all down the seaward side.

I sat in a pew halfway down the church, on the right, where we always used to sit. My mind filled with pictures. Mum's wheelchair parked at the end of the pew, Dad at the front, Albert who smelt of tobacco and gave me chewing gum, turning round to give me a secret wink (even he was dead now), Reg Bennett, smiling – always smiling – me as a little kid, standing on the seat, clapping. Mum's coffin, strewn with flowers… I began to cry. There was no reason to fight it. The tears came in torrents, running down my face and splattering onto my jeans. As I cried, I felt again the sensation from my dream of the white sheet tearing, and the eagle disappearing from view. The feeling of letting go.

On the wall at the front of the church there is a crucifix, carved from white marble, leaning out from the wall, with its tortured eyes turned downwards towards the floor. The Sunday before Mum died it looked like wax – so pale – so much like a dead thing. Maybe it was just the way the light caught it. Maybe it was what Clare had said about waxworks. I'd hurried out of church, out into the light, out into the sunshine, feeling sick. Now the crucifix was bathed in yellow sunlight and the white stone seemed to glow with warmth, as though it would be soft to touch. As though it were alive. Suffering, but alive. Feeling.

I wiped my face on the sleeve of my jumper. There was

a Bible on the shelf in front of me. I turned to the contents page at the front and leafed through the strange names. What was it? Ecc-le-si-as-tes. That was it: page 653. I opened the book and found the page. There it was. The poem I'd heard on the beach.

'For everything a time and a season... a time to weep and a time to laugh... a time to mourn and a time to dance... a time to die and a time to be born...'

I sat for a moment reading the words over and over and then, as if from nowhere – from somewhere far outside of me – I had an unexplainable feeling of joy – as if I would burst if I didn't dance or sing or run or hug somebody. It only lasted a minute – it was like a sudden intense light – so bright and so deep that it almost hurt – like a laser burning into me – changing me...

I hung the key back on the hook in Dad's study and whistled for Wombat. The sea is smoother now and the wind has dropped. Down on the beach the crowds are gathering. I can see children leaping about on the bouncy castle, rocking its spongy cushions from side to side in the sand. The sun feels warm on my back. I have pulled my hoody off and knotted it round my waist. Wombat is pulling hard on his lead, sniffing at tufts of sandy grass that sprout along the sides of the slope. I am smiling like an idiot and I have a sense of things about to happen...

I can see yellow T-shirts and the banner stretched out beside the hot dog stall, and four white-faced figures standing in a line. As my feet reach the soft white sand I can hear a saxophone begin to play and now I can hear the words again, through the strains of the sad melody.

'There is a time for everything...'

All Lion books are available from your local
bookshop, or can be ordered via our website
or from Marston Book Services. For a free
catalogue, showing the complete list of titles
available, please contact:

Customer Services
Marston Book Services
PO Box 269
Abingdon
Oxon
OX14 4YN

Tel: 01235 465500
Fax: 01235 465555

Our website can be found at:
www.lionhudson.com

If you want to know more about
Sue Mayfield's books, see her website:
www.suemayfield.com